SPIRITO SPLENDIDO

SPIRITO SPLENDIDO

Too Precocious For Purgatory

Dee Schore

✝ Divine Mercy Press ✝

Please Note: This book is a memoir of growing up during the years of WWII. Every effort has been made by the author and publisher to insure the accuracy of these memories. However, some allowance must be made for human error.

The theological ideas expressed herein are not necessarily those of Divine Mercy Press or its staff.

1.   Cataloging in Publication data
2.   Schore, Dee
3.   Spirito Splendido: Too Precocious For   Purgatory/by
        Dee Schore
4.   p.   cm.
5.   ISBN 0-978-0-9755471-9-9

Back cover adult photo courtesy EWP

"How Would You Like To Kiss Me In the Moonlight?" by Harold Adamson, reprinted with permission from Warner Chapel. "Leprosy" and "Reveille" appear to be in the public domain

✟ **Divine Mercy Press** ✟
1973 Apple Street, #35, Oceanside, California 92054
5319 Willis Avenue, Dallas, Texas 75206

Acknowledgements

This book began as an attempt to preserve my family history for my granddaughter, Nicole. The more I wrote, well, the more I wrote. The more my friends read, the more stories they wanted to read. One friend in particular, Elizabeth Westbrook Pirkey, asked if she could read the stories to her dear friend Crosby. This wonderful eighty-nine year old gentleman, who had been a writer since he was sixteen years old, agreed to be my editor. Crosby had taught a university class in memoir writing and found my style intriguing. He encouraged me to write in the vernacular from the perspective of a precocious young girl and preserve the richness of my history, no matter how raunchy or simplistic. I wish to thank Crosby Holden and Elizabeth Westbrook Pirkey.

To the staff of Divine Mercy Press and Elaine Sauter, who have been generous with their time and talents: thanks to all of you. I am indebted to Pat Hildebrand, for her careful editing.

Thanks also to Sgt. Ronald Orange, USMC, for his help on the rights to *Reveille*.

To those of you who read advanced copies and encouraged me to continue writing so that you can continue laughing, I thank you.

—DS

To
Nicole Angelina Jeter

Table of Contents

Introduction

The voices in this book are idiosyncratic, and rightly so, in order to support the genre. My parents had the behavior of repeating, in strong New York accents, all of the stories you are about to read, and you will understand why it is with keen memory, that I would tell you what I recall, growing up as a child who was, as the title bears, too precocious for Purgatory.

The manner in which this book is written preserves the memory of what was heard and seen, which if not honored, would cause me to lose part of my history; and, in a way, yours. These memories live in storytelling. We should all tell our stories and plant historical markers along our paths. Some of my stories will, no doubt, trigger your own and even though you may never tell the story you recall to anyone else, just remembering it will enrich you as you search and remember your roots.

The timeline is the best I can remember, and it could not have been possible without military documents which my father had archived from his first to his final day in the Marine Corps. One afternoon while writing, I found myself wishing out loud, that I had access to these documents that would substantiate the dates and places of his service. A strong motivation came over me to leave my desk and go rummage through the garage. There, in a green locker box, was a file containing not only the documents, but photographs and memorabilia that I had not seen since I was a very young child.

I encourage all of you to open that trunk; the one in your attic, garage, storage locker, or perhaps it's simply an old shoebox.

Go ahead.

Open it.

Remember.

Dee Schore
August 2006

Dee and Mae

In the beginning. . . .

my mother said, "Ya were born with a silver spoon in ya mouth, but it wasn't our spoon."

I still remember her with her strong New York accent starting our conversation with that opening sentence and stressing each word with a wave of the cigarette held daintily between her fingers.

I was five years old at the time. It opens a door to a sacred space, the recollection of what I describe as the "Once Upon a Time" portal.

We sat opposite each other, having coffee and Italian cookies, at a large oak dining table in the kitchen of my grandmother's home in Corona, New York. We lived in this elegant home with Grandma Catherine Sidoti Canale, Auntie Olympia and Aunt Yolanda until my father, a career Marine, returned from Japan in 1946.

The usual topics of conversation around the dining table included Mussolini, movies, fashion, books, Sicily and Italy.

On that particular day in 1946, the topic was my mother's perception of who I was and what my destiny could be.

Mom continued, "It's a sayin'. 'She was born with a silver spoon in her mouth.'" She lit a cigarette and removed a bit of tobacco from her lip with a well-manicured fingernail.

I looked up as I removed my silver spoon from my coffee noticing the pattern on the handle as I gently laid it on the saucer. Though well-worn, it was cherished by my great grandmother in Florence, Italy and had traveled by ship to America with Grandma Catherine sometime before my Mother was born in 1918.

"What does it mean?" I asked.

"The spoon is a symbol. It symbolizes the person was born with means—usually money, but also opportunity."

"What opportunity?" I asked sipping my coffee.

"The opportunity ta get an education, learn etiquette, know the finer things in life," Mom explained in an exasperated tone.

"Look, have a cookie, Dee. What I'm tryin' ta say is that ya don't act like anybody else in our family. I'm just tellin' ya this for ya own good."

I looked at her stunned, not stunned by what she was saying but because she had figured out that I was different; a thought that had occurred to me on many occasions.

After another long, deep drag on her cigarette, Mom said, "For instance . . ." She paused leaning her chin into the palm of one hand; the other held the smoldering stick, which jettisoned embers onto the oak table, making another tattoo for posterity.

"This is the way I see it. It's like ya were born inta' another family, in another part a the country ten years ago only ya not ten."

"I'm only five," I answered defiantly.

"I know ya five. Ya act like ya much older. And another point: Where did ya learn to mix blouses, skirts and sweaters up ta make ya day-ta'-day clothes look like costumes? And, what's with borrowin' my jewelry? This isn't playin' pretend. This is ya real life!"

"I don't want to look like everybody else," I replied, looking down at the napkin in my lap and folding it neatly while my Mother ignored my plea.

"The topper is, Dee, ya don't tauk like the rest of us. Ya tauk Hollywood English, but ya don't live in Hollywood. How did it happen that ya don't have the New York brogue as the Irish say? Ya have ta admit, there are a lot a questions here that we can't answer."

"Mom, you know I went to movies with Aunt Yola and saw them over and over again and memorized the words and songs. I—"

Mom interrupted, "I neva knew anybody, kid or grown-up, who does the things ya do. How are we goin' ta explain this ta ya father when he comes home from the war?"

"I don't know. I'm just me," I answered.

Mom looked off into space like she used to do when she'd sit on Jones Beach and stare at the ocean. She was thinking. I was quiet.

"Ya know, kid," she said with a sigh, "what if we just tell ya father that Amelia Earhart would have neva flown her airplane if her parents had told her she couldn't be a free thinka'."

This conversation was a moment of truth for me. The silver spoon in my mouth did not belong to the Canale or Sauter family. I *was* different. I don't know how it happened; it simply evolved from imagination, having very little fear and perceiving my actions as alternatives to a group mentality.

I am still, today, living my truth as my reality. The vignettes in this book are memories that formed these truths. My hope is that the reader will celebrate the differences among children; rather than forcing them into a mold of how they should act, learn and respond to external influences.

I do not condone the idea of a huge melting pot of humanity where individuality is suppressed and we act like androids. Many an artist is cloaked in moments of lunacy and irrationality in the privacy of their own psyche. Perhaps these moments may serve as a portal to a new style of painting or music. It may promote the birth of an entrepreneur, or an African American or woman as President of the United States. Why not give the fidgeting child some time to dance, stomp, babble, sing, or paint at an appropriate time and place? Can we not as parents and teachers guide children to their place of safety where creativity can be nurtured and respect for humanity and all living creatures be held in high esteem?

May the ideas, which begin in childhood, become the silver spoons of opportunity that nurture their splendid spirits.

Dee and Aunt Yola

Grandma Catherine Sidoti Canale

I, Boo, Beep

I come from a family of characters: funny, crazy, sometimes hysterical. If it's true that we choose our families somewhere between spirit and the sperm hitting the egg; then I picked a good fit. I see myself a product of my heritage: Northern Italian, Sicilian, and German, as well as my environment that changed geographical location frequently. My parents, though born in the United States of America, like many born around 1918 in New York, are of solid ethnic heritage. From the neighborhood of Corona, New York, comes my mother, Amelia Helen Canale. Amelia, Americanized to "Mae" by her peers, is the third born after her brothers Eugene and Phillip.

She has a younger sister, Yolanda, ("Yola"). Though I do not have much interaction with my uncles, I spend many hours of my young life witnessing the emotionally charged exchanges between my Mom and

Aunt Yola. Their voices, speaking in Italian, are often held at a fever pitch, punctuated with the Italian hand salute which translates to "Up your goolie."

I meet my Mom when she is 23 years old. The year is 1941—the year of the Pearl Harbor attack. When I'm older, I think Mom resembles an Italian movie star with dark auburn hair and hazel eyes. Later in my life I consider her a cross between Sophia Loren and Gina Lollabrigita—sensual and ballsy.

Unlike our other family members, I always see her dressed up like a model in a magazine. She looks like a knockout even the first thing in the morning. She makes breakfast in freshly applied makeup and wears her hair pulled up on top of her head; the waves of curls held by a silk scarf from a fancy department store in Manhattan. She's dressed in an ecru satin robe with topstitched trim on the collar and cuffs. Her pajamas are ones that could be coveted by Katherine Hepburn. On her feet are ermine trimmed mules with her pedicured toes peeking out.

A Lucky Strike cigarette dangles from her perfectly made up lips on which she applies Revlon's Jungle Red lipstick. On her Sicilian olive-toned skin, she powder puffs Coty powder and rouge; her perfume: Evening In Paris. She wears the scent not because she loves it, but because Dad has sent her a large gift box filled with the entire line—soap, perfume, dusting powder, toilet water and sachet. I say *sent*, because he is in the Marine Corps and on duty somewhere in China. The black market stretched from Paris to Shanghai by late 1943, the year I begin experiencing the vignettes that make me the free spirit I will become.

The only way I know where I was living prior to this moment is from dates on old photographs. I am now living in Corona, New York with my maternal Grandmother Catherine, her sister Auntie Olympia, Aunt Yola and my Mom.

Mom and I visit my paternal grandparents in Brooklyn and we take photos of us together with the German side of the family. Contrasting the Sicilian side of the family, they are sweet and calm. I wonder, "What's wrong with these people?" I have a feeling that my Mom feels repressed and can't really express her feelings with the Sauter family. The Sauters speak calmly and quietly. The Canales yell and cuss.

Mom works for Lowe's Theaters as the head cashier. She gets up every day, dresses in her fine clothes and takes the subway to work. I watch her walk away from the front gate and it makes me cry.

I am stuck at home with Grandma Catherine and Auntie Olympia (eighty two years old and counting). Grandma writes a newspaper column about herbal remedies for the *Il Progresso* newspaper and often writes poetry under the pen name of Minerva de la Sclera. To keep busy and earn money, Auntie sews beads on evening purses. These days the motto is, "Children Should Be Seen And Not Heard." I obey, never speaking unless I am spoken to. It's all right. I'm becoming a keen observer.

Mom comes home around five o'clock with stories about different situations at work. She paints a grim picture of someone getting hired who dresses like a "schlub" (whatever that is), or someone getting "PG" (whatever that is), or someone mouthing off to the manager. That someone would end up always getting fired. She loves to tell Aunt Yola these stories because it makes Mom look like "hot stuff." Nothing interesting ever happens around Aunt Yola. She acts disinterested at first, rolls her eyes, and says, "Get outta' here, Mae!"

Several times, I walk into the living room to hear Mom ranting about some 'incompetent tart' who had mouthed off at the boss.

"She had a mouth on her I tell ya," she says with a cigarette flopping around between her lips like a piece of loose spaghetti. "She didn't say I, boo, beep, . . ." She stops in mid sentence when she sees me coming like maybe there's some secret ending.

I kind of like the saying. I adopt it at first, quietly, to myself, "I, boo, beep. I, boo, beep." I turn it into a song and add some fancy hip movements. Then I start singing out loud, with the choreography. After awhile I notice Aunt Yola gets awfully angry at my song and dance routine. I can't figure out why until one day I hear the story of Lillian Blonski while I'm hiding behind the living room drapes.

Arriving home, Mom says, "Hey, Yo, (as she refers to Aunt Yola). I got a hot one for ya. Ya heard me tauk 'bout Lil Blonski from work? Seems she got caught with her hand in the till with the seven o'clock "take" a *The Mummy's Curse*, the Lon Chaney film."

"By the way, Yo, Dee should neva be allowed to see that one. It'll scare the ya know what outta' her."

"Anyway, Lil got caught by my manager, Mr. Liberman. He grabbed her by the wrist yellin', 'Give it up, sister!' Well, ol' Lil stood there with a fist full a dollar bills. She didn't say, "I, boo, beep, kiss my ass or nothin'." She threw the money on the floor, jerked her arm loose and walked outta' Lowe's like the Queen a Sheba."

"Ah, Mae, get outta' here!" says Aunt Yola.

This is a moment of enlightenment for me. I now know something right up there with the meaning of life, why a dead person goes to Purgatory, where babies come from and why you should change your underwear before you go out of the house. I'm now one of them; but they don't know that I have the understanding of at least one of their secret winks, nods, and giggles.

At that moment, both of them see me hiding behind the draperies. My shoes are sticking out from under the velvet pleats, but like an ostrich I think I'm invisible. I'm mouthing, "I, boo, beep, kiss my ass! I boo, beep, kiss my goolie," and swaying my hips to the rhythm of the words. It's kind of a reversal of sitting in the audience and watching the show.

With my discovery comes Mom's declaration, "No more I, boo, beep for ya, young lady. Hang up those dancin' shoes along with the little ditty."

What they don't know is from this time on, the phrase *I, boo, beep, kiss my ass/goolie or nothin'*, becomes a three-and-a-half-year-old's mantra.

Grandpa Lorenzo Canale

Auntie Olympia Sidoti

The Dinner Guest

I never miss daily Mass while I'm living in New York. That's pretty good for a kid of not even four years old. Auntie Olympia and I walk a few blocks to Our Lady of Perpetual Headache Catholic church. That's what I call it. As we walk, Auntie remains silent, but I recite a Hail Mary, in English, in my head. Auntie taught me these. She speaks really good Italian, but she doesn't speak English very well.

> *Hail Mary full of grapes. The load is with you. Blessed art thou amuck us women and blessed is the fruit of my groom. Cheese and rice.*

If I get tired of saying that one, I throw in the Lord's Prayer.

*Our Father wick art and haven. Hall of
wed bee thy game. Thy king and come.
Thy willa bee done. On earth aspen
heaven.*

This morning I am walking fast because it's cold
and windy. I see a big dog crossing the street. I get a
little scared. I pray under my breath,

*Yeah though I walk through the belly of
the shadow of death, I will not fear
Evelyn.*

This is part of the 23rd song, I think.

We walk inside the chapel and dip our first two
fingers into the Holy Water. We make the sign of the
cross and walk to the front pew. We always sit there. It's
usually only crowded on Sundays, which is today, but I
guess with the bad weather people are staying home.

I love the smell of incense and candle wax. I light
a candle for my Dad. This is tricky. He's Lutheran and
doesn't know I come here. Mom told me not to tell. As I
light the candle I say a prayer that he'll be safe while
he's at the war. It has worked so far. I'm a true believer.
I guess he doesn't have to know I do this as long as
Jesus hears the prayer.

We sit through the Latin Mass. I don't
understand what Father Mike is saying, but I love being
here.

There are two huge angels on either side of the altar. They have wings that stretch from above their heads and down to the floor. I guess they're made out of marble. I've never touched them because I'm not allowed to go near the altar. They seem to stare at me.

Father Mike has just finished communion and gives us a blessing in Latin. I hear thunder and some people get up to leave the church. Another big crack of thunder comes and the angel in front of me is glowing with light. I rub my eyes because I see this "thing," this well . . . angel floating down and standing right in front of me. It kind of comes and goes. It's a little hard to explain since it changes. It's kind of like looking at a fish under water. One moment this angel is a little blurry and then it changes to a solid form, but not like marble. It looks like a real person. It's very big and very . . .well . . .scary. I want to say, "Jesus, Mary and Joseph," which is kind of like cussing which my Mom says I can do silently, but not out loud. This should be an exception. I mumble it under my breath and hope Jesus won't be offended.

I look at Auntie. I can tell she doesn't see what I'm seeing. The angel is standing right in front of me. We leave the pew and walk down the aisle towards the door. We dip into the Holy Water again on our way out of the church and bless ourselves. I turn around for one last look at the angel. She's standing right behind me. I smell something I've never smelled before, a smell of flowers mixed with herbs, and the smell of a thunderstorm; all wrapped into one wonderful smell. Like when Mom grinds coffee beans, only better.

Auntie takes me by the hand and tells me we'd better hurry up since it's going to rain. I turn and look in back of me. The angel is still there. When we stop at the street corner, she stops. When we walk, she walks. I have trouble walking forward because I want to keep looking at her. I'm saying "her," but I can't really tell if it's a girl or a boy. Her feet look big, like a man's feet. Maybe this is a man, a beautiful man. Whatever he is, his face is so sweet. I have never seen anything like it that's real flesh and blood.

I turn to look again. The wings are so big! It must be easy to fly with those things. There is a sound I haven't heard before. It's like the sound of wind through feathers—not a flapping really, more like the rustling of a pinwheel in a gentle breeze.

Auntie startles me with, "What's a matta' you? What you look at? No turn arounda. Walk! *Andiamo.* We be late."

I stop. "Auntie, I have to tell you something. There's somebody following us."

Looking behind us she says, "Non. No body dare."

"Look again," I demand.

We stop. She glances around and she looks at me. "Who's a dare?"

I whisper, "It's an angel from Mass. It floated down from the altar."

"You got-a big-a magination for a leetle girl. You wanna angel? You tell-a Grandma."

"Tell Grandma? Oh, no! We barely talk to each other. How do I tell her?"

"Dats-a you problem. No mine," says Auntie.

We walk without speaking another word. I hear the sound of the pinwheel. We enter the backdoor of our house and walk into the kitchen where Grandma is cooking the one o'clock meal we call dinner.

"Hail da fateful!" says Grandma. "Fateful" is as close as she can get to "faithful." "How's-a Father Michael?"

Auntie and I stand there. We don't speak. Auntie shoves me towards Grandma. "Go. Tell-a you story."

"Well? Como, como . . .what?" asks Grandma looking up from stirring the pasta sauce with a wooden spoon. The spoon Mom said she always got spanked with. I get really scared now.

"I brought someone home for dinner."

"Who's-a dat?" asks Grandma. At this point, she takes her eyes off me and looks up about seven feet off the floor, to my left and behind me.

"It's an angel." I can't believe I'm telling her, but if I don't, I'll be in big trouble. The worst thing you can do in this household is not answer a question.

She keeps looking upward. She must be able to see what I can see!

"What's-a ees name?"

"I don't know," I answer.

"Ask," she says raising her voice.

I turn around and I see Auntie standing with her head hung low as if she's going to get yelled at after Grandma is finished with me.

I look way, way up above me and ask out loud, "What is your name?" At that moment, I see lights sparkling off of the wings and a glow come from deep inside of the angel. I hear the name Gabriel. I don't know if anyone else in the room that's human hears it, but I do.

I turn to Grandma Catherine. "He said, 'Gabriel'."

Grandma turns to continue cooking our dinner. "Well, donna' be-a rude. Putta' a place atta' da table. Eee's-a always welcome." She raises the wooden cooking spoon in the air, which translates to, "I don't want to hear anymore."

I set the table, which is my only job. I'm not sure where to set the extra place and I'm too afraid to ask Grandma. I set an extra napkin and silverware next to my place. Gabriel hovers in the corner. Auntie slinks out of the room mumbling something about how I'm in for it when my Mom comes home.

Within the hour Mom, Aunt Yola, our friends Aunt Rose and Aunt Lolly arrive for the main meal of the day. Grandma hasn't spoken to me. I have not left the kitchen because I don't want to leave Gabriel alone.

The last one to arrive is Grandpa Canale. I don't know him very well. He is in the restaurant business. He is only allowed to come and eat dinner with us once a week, usually on Sundays. He has to be gone by suppertime and never sleeps at our house. His side of the family is related to the Gambino family. Grandma Catherine and Mom have explained to me that it's safer for Grandpa to just visit because of his ties to another family called the Mafia. Because we are a Catholic family, Grandpa and Grandma will never divorce. Out of his sense of duty, she says, he supports the household with money and food.

The greeting is loud with hugs and kisses on cheeks. Grandma orders everyone to sit down. The women are so busy talking they don't notice the extra place setting; but Grandpa does.

"Do you have a guest, Catherine?" he says to Grandma.

I'm terrified. I know she's going to ask me to explain. Thoughts fill my head. My Mom will laugh if I tell who's here and Aunt Yola will tease me for the rest of my life. Aunt Lolly will say I'm a crazy person. Aunt Rose will tell my Mom how sorry she feels for *her*. Aunt Olympia will never mention another word about it and probably never take me to Mass again because she'll think I'll steal the crucifix. A person might think it's a really good experience—to see an angel— but to me this is the worst experience of my life. What if my Dad finds out? Then he'll know I go to Mass—oh, I'm doomed; doomed for lying, doomed for pretending. I'M GOING TO HELL! No Purgatory for me. I'll go right to Hell. I'm sick. I've wasted my life. Grandma interrupts my lament. This is the first time I have ever heard her speak English so clearly.

"Dee has-a brought-a da Archangel Gabriel home from-a Mass. Eee's a welcome here-a anytime." She picks up the big wooden serving spoon. The spoon has divots in it from hitting Mom and Aunt Yola when they were little. She wags the spoon at my Mom who looks shocked but is just about to laugh. She clams up.

Grandma continues in a loud voice, "Eef anyone of-a ju' makes-a fun a da child, ju'll half-a ta answer ta me. We will-a no' speak a dis again."

I have never seen my Grandma stand up for anybody. I glance at her and somehow she looks very different to me. She looks at me and her face looks sweet.

There is a cloud of quiet over the table. It looks like a wake only nobody's crying. Grandma blesses herself and nods to Grandpa who says, "*Vino?*" Well, by this time we all need a drink.

The first glass Grandpa fills is Gabriel's. He never broke this habit until the day he died.

Dee

Dee and Aunt Yola

My English Teachers

I want to learn to speak English properly.

Living with a bunch of women who speak Italian most of the time is not a very good way to learn.

At the house in Corona, New York where I spent most of my pre-school years, I learn to cook in Italian, iron in Italian, food shop in Italian and negotiate, yes, in Italian.

My Mom is at work all day and she speaks English to me in the evening. If her sister, my Aunt Yola, comes over for supper, I hear them speaking English to each other and Italian to everyone else. Grandma Catherine and Auntie Olympia speak Italian and very little English. They are my caretakers when Mom and Aunt Yola are at work. I copy how the nuns talk at church. They speak good English, but I won't be going to Catholic school to learn more from them.

I'm sure my Dad could teach me some real English, but he's overseas at the war. You can see my dilemma. If I want to learn English, and I do, I'm going to have to find a teacher. I need to find one before we move to a military base and I have to begin first grade.

"Mom," I ask, "do you think you could teach me really good English?"

"Wadda' ya taukin' about? Ya tauk good English auready."

"I mean I want to talk like the people I hear on the radio at night; the ones who tell us the news. I want to talk with good dictation."

Mom looks at me puzzled, "I guess ya mean diction. Why do ya wanna tauk like Edward R. Morrow when ya can tauk like Walter Winchell or Edward G. Robinson?"

She does an impression of Edward G. Robinson as Public Enemy #1. "You dirty rat! Yeah!"

I realize that one problem I'll have learning from Mom is that I'll have to dangle a cigarette from the side of my mouth like she always does. I can see I'm getting nowhere fast. I approach the subject with Aunt Yola.

"Aunt Yola. I want to learn to speak English."

"Ya mean like a Limey?" she asks.

"No. Not English . . . English, . . . American English."

"Why? Ya tauk good," she answers.

"Yeah, but I wanna talk better than I do. Can you help me?"

She stares at me, nodding her head and says, "OK. The best way ta learn English is at the movies. Ya can come ta work with me at Lowe's. I'll be workin' the candy counter for the matinees and I can sneak ya in. Ya mother won't know we're there. She'll be makin' the rounds a' the theaters for the audit next week. We'll start then. Grandma and Auntie will be glad ta see ya outta' the house."

"Will Mom think it's a good idea to go to work with you, Aunt Yola?" I ask.

Aunt Yola thinks for a moment. "No. We won't tell her. She goes ta work early and gets home late. I'm only there from one o'clock until five o'clock. We'll be home in plenty a time. I'll tell Grandma we're plannin' a special surprise for ya mother and not ta tell her that we have ta go out every day for a few days."

"Oh boy! I get to see a movie every day?"

"Yeah. The one that's playin' tomorrow is the *Princess and the Pirate* with Bob Hope and Virginia Mayo. Ya heard ya Mother tauk about 'em, haven't ya?"

"Oh, yes! Mom says I look a little bit like Miss Mayo. She told me how funny Bob Hope is too," I answer excitedly.

"Well, kid, pay attention and y'll learn somethin'. Ya know, I think ya tauk different from the rest a us already."

"This is great! I have two new English teachers— Miss Mayo and Bob Hope! Has Mom seen *Princess and the Pirate*? Have you, Aunt Yola?"

"Ya mother has done nothin' but work on the audit for two weeks. I seen some of it when I don't have customers at the counter."

The next day Mom leaves for work. She's the head cashier at Lowe's and she's nervous about the audit. She kisses me goodbye and tells me to mind my elders. I do what Aunt Yola tells me to do. I get dressed, fix my hair, and have some pastina cereal for breakfast. We leave just after noon because we have to take the subway and be at work by one o'clock.

"I'm going to be taught how to talk by two famous movie stars. I'm very lucky!" I say to Aunt Yola.

"Sure, kid," says Aunt Yola as she puts on her coat and helps me with mine. "I hope ya don't change ya accent too much. I won't recognize ya."

"Maybe I'll just learn how to talk and save it for when I go to school."

"I don't think so, kid. Y'll have ta practice. Mr. Hope and Miss Mayo speak Hollywood English. It's as close ta perfect as ya can get," she answers.

We arrive at the theater. There's a big poster about the movie. Aunt Yola reads it to me, "*The Princess and the Pirate* starring Bob Hope and Virginia Mayo. Metro Goldwyn Mayer. The Goldwyn Girls. In Technicolor."

Excitedly I say, "And they all speak Hollywood English!"

The poster shows Bob Hope dressed like a pirate and Miss Mayo in a beautiful blue dress.

Aunt Yola hangs up our coats and we walk on the beautiful red carpet to the candy counter. She turns on the light inside the glass case.

"Wow! Do we get to eat candy too, Aunt Yola?"

"Sure, kid. Help yourself ta a candy bar. The show is gonna start in about fifteen minutes. I'll show ya where ta sit now, because I may get a customer. It's been slow lately, but maybe it'll be busier today."

I pick out a big, chocolate candy bar. This is a treat! I love chocolate. I never see these at home. We only have the Torrone almond candy from Italy. Aunt Yola takes me into the theater and I sit in the first seat in the back row.

"I'll come in ta check on ya every few minutes. If it's slow I can sit with ya for a little while," she says.

This is the best! I'm sitting at the movies just like a grown up! I'm going to learn how to talk like they do in Hollywood. The lights dim. The heavy, red curtain on the stage opens. A picture of a big lion comes on the screen. It roars. I roar back. I'm at the movies! It's in Technicolor! The chair feels really good. I like the texture of the fabric. This is the happiest day of my life! I want to do this every day!

Aunt Yola comes in and reads the title on the screen, "'Costumes by Mary Grant.' Ya gonna love this. Have fun and I'll see ya later. I think ya the only one in the audience."

The movie starts. There is a bad pirate named Hook. He steals a ship called the *Mary Ann*. Virginia Mayo is Princess Margaret who has run away from home because she wants to marry a man who her father doesn't like. That's kinda like my Mom marrying my Dad. Grandma didn't like him at first because he wasn't Italian, but it's all right with her now.

Virginia Mayo and I have the same color hair, blonde, and she has curls just like me too. She is very beautiful! She stands up very straight and walks as if she's floating. I guess that's what Mom means when she says to walk and not bounce. I wonder if Miss Mayo has to practice walking with a book on her head like I do.

Bob Hope is Sylvester the Great. He plays an actor with a lot of costumes who puts on shows. He's funny and says things to Miss Mayo like, "Sit down and take a load off." That's funny. I want to speak just like Miss Mayo, but I want a nose and sense of humor like Mr. Hope.

I'm paying attention to every word and I hope I can remember later so I can practice and get really good at this Hollywood English.

I love Princess Margaret's words, "Tell this filthy cutthroat to take his hands off me!" she says to pirate Hook. I repeat the line again. Then she says to Sylvester, "Please forgive me for thinking you a coward." I repeat a lot of what she says exactly the way she says it.

"Sylvester, come here. Sit by me. Why did you expose yourself to such danger for me?" asks Miss Mayo.

I repeat it with the same voice and tone. I don't care what the answer is. I just love the question.

My favorite line Miss Mayo says is, "Because of love, I disobeyed my father and ran out on one of the noblest families in Europe." I love this! I repeat it again and again to make sure I can remember it.

They escape from the pirate ship and go to the Boar's Head Inn. The lady who owns the place smokes a pipe. I never saw a girl smoke a pipe before.

They stay at the inn and find costumes to wear. They plan to earn money at the theater by dancing and singing. In the audience are a lot of men who act drunk and tough.

Sylvester is scared. He sends Miss Mayo, who is now Princess Margaret as far as I'm concerned, out onto the stage.

She leaves his side saying, "I am of royal blood. There's a price on my head."

I love this line! I make it my own. I repeat it out loud several times to make sure I say it exactly the way Princess Margaret does. I hold my head high and pull my shoulders back just like she's teaching me.

She is dressed in a costume that looks like the one I have in my storybook of Rapunzel, but instead of looking like the princess, she looks like the prince. I'd like to be a prince one day.

Princess Margaret goes on stage because the men don't like Sylvester very much. She just stands there and before she sings, the men like her a lot.

They clap and scream and throw money. I think they like her costume, because she is just standing there acting nervous. She starts singing. This is the first song I learn from the movies.

> *"How would you like to kiss me in the*
> *moonlight?*
> *"How would you like to hold me in*
> *your arms?*
> *"I got what you want.*
> *"You got what I want.*
> *"So what are we waiting for?*

Because she sings so well, the men throw a lot of money on the stage. She and Sylvester pick it up and have money to travel on a good ship to return home.

Well, in the end her father shows up on the boat and says it's all right to marry the guy who's not very rich. The princess runs to the man she loves who just happens to be on the same boat because he was worried that the pirate kidnapped her and he came to save her. Sylvester thinks he's the one she loves, but she walks past him saying, "Sorry, Sylvester, I want a younger man."

I ask Aunt Yola who the man is she kisses. She says it's a joke. It's Bing Crosby. I don't get it.

Well, would you believe it? I get to see it again before we have to go home. This is good because I can practice the lines of the princess.

Aunt Yola and I take the subway home, and she tells me that in real life Bob Hope doesn't drink beer so they put apple juice in a glass and add cream to make pretend beer for the scene where he drinks four glasses of beer.

She asks, "Did ya learn some good English?"

I answer slowly and deliberately, "I am of royal blood. There is a price on my head."

"Oh, brother! Ya better can that accent before ya mother gets home."

"Tell this filthy cutthroat to take his hands off me!" I say curtly.

"Ah, Jesus, Mary and Joseph. We're in trouble!"

"Are you a man or a mouse?" I say just like Bob Hope.

"Ya *will* stop this before we get home, won't ya?" Aunt Yola asks looking worried.

We're home an hour before Mom arrives. She comes home exhausted from a hard day's work. I'm full of energy.

"Hi, honey. How was ya day? What did ya do?" Mom asks.

Aunt Yola looks at me in horror as if she knows what I'm going to say.

I open my mouth to say, "Sit down and take a load off."

Aunt Yola lifts me up and gives me a kiss on the cheek to shut me up. It works this time, but she realizes that she can't police me forever.

I start kissing her cheek singing, "How would you like to kiss me in the moonlight?"

Mom's jaw drops open. "Did ya make that up? It's good. Don't ya think it's good, Yola?"

I continue singing, "How would you like to hold me in your arms?"

Aunt Yola looks horrified.

"I got what you want. You got what I want."

Mom falls into a chair. "Where does she come up with these things?"

By this time I'm singing as loud as I can, "So what are we waiting for?"

Yola says, "She's got a wild imagination, Mae."

"I think she gets it from her father. Ya know, he's got that wacky sense a humor," says Mom.

"Dee, ya voice sounds different. Who are ya supposed ta be?"

"I'm the queen of all the little jacks. I'm a card," I say imitating Bob Hope.

Mom answers while yawning, "And I'm just tired enough ta believe ya."

Mae, Steve, Steve, and Steve
Or
Mae, Dee, Grandpa Albert Sauter, Grandma
Victoria Sauter

We're All Steve

Sometimes Mom tells me it's time to visit my Dad's parents, Grandma and Grandpa Steve. They live in Flatbush, Brooklyn, New York, on 64th Place. This side of the family is German, but Grandma and Grandpa were born in Brooklyn. It's a good thing for me that they speak English. Well, they speak "Brooklyn" which is even better. It's funny. Their real names are Victoria and Albert Sauter, but I call them Grandma and Grandpa Steve because I have nicknamed myself Steve and I want them to be Steves too. This is Grandpa's suggestion. Yup, we're all Steve.

It's a little bit like the Three Stooges because when one of us talks, then the other two answer.

"Hey, here's Steve," says Grandpa Steve.

"Hello, Steve," I say.

"Hello, Steve," comes their reply in unison.

Boy, this keeps a person on their toes. Once in awhile two of us give different answers.

"Do ya want milk and cake, Steve?" Grandma looks at both of us.

"Yes, please," I answer.

"Yes, Grandma Steve, but make it 'cawfee' with my cake," says Grandpa.

The fact that Grandpa Steve allows me to pick my own nickname means a lot to me. No other adults or kids I know have changed their first names. Where is their creativity? Don't they go beyond fantasy? Can't they change a moniker now and then? I'll bet it's because the family won't go along with the idea, but this family encourages me. I've got a great life here being Steve.

Whenever we're in Brooklyn, Mom doesn't stop me from using my alias and thinks it adds to my creativity. We don't use it at Spaghetti-ville as I call my house in Corona.

After we have our food, Mom and Grandma Steve do the dishes. Grandpa Steve and I go down to the basement to talk about life and other important stuff. The women talk about baking and my Dad, who's somewhere overseas.

Grandpa Steve gives me great advice, "If ya change ya name, ya can be anythin' ya want other than a drunkard, thief or forcator."

I know what the first two are, but I never heard of a "forcator."

"What's a forcator?"

"I'll tell ya when ya older, but not now because ya won't know what I'm talkin' about."

"Give me a hint, Grandpa Steve,"

"Ah, Jesus, Steve. I'm sorry I brought up the whole i-dear."

"Does it mean I'm 'for' something that's called a 'cator'?" I'm staring at him and he's opening his cigar box and not answering.

"Ya know somethin', Steve? I got a better i-dear. Let's have a cigar."

"OK, Steve," I reply. "Do I get to wear the band on my finger so I have a ring?"

"Sure, Steve. It's part a havin' a cigar."

Grandpa Steve lights his cigar and I just hold mine pretending to smoke.

"I got ya somethin' really special. I want ya ta keep it forever and pass it on ta ya grandchildren. Never sell it or trade it no madder what's happenin' in ya life. If ya down on ya luck and don't know where ya next meal is comin' from—don't sell it. Ya gotta promise me, Steve." He looks very serious.

"I promise, Grandpa Steve. I promise. I'll keep it forever until the day I die, and I'll leave it to my grandchildren."

He opens his wallet and pulls out a business card. He reads the front of the card, "The New York Central Railroad Company. H. E. Miller Interline and Pullman. Ticket Seller. Ticket Office Grand Central Terminal New York, N.Y. Telephone Murray Hill 8000 Extension 279."

I look at him puzzled.

He turns over the card. On the back is written the name, *Babe Ruth*.

Grandpa Steve continues, "Dis' guy, Babe Ruth, neva quits. No madder how bad a day he's havin'. No madder if he's sick. No madder if he just lost his best friend, all his money, his dog. He's no quitter. Always remember 'im."

"Does he work for the railroad?" I ask.

"Ah, Jesus, Steve. I worry about ya. Ain't ya gettin' no education? The Babe plays baseball. I got dis' here from him for ya. He wrote his name fa ya on dis' card because it was the only piece a' paper I had. It's my brudder's card."

Grandpa Steve hands me the card like it's more precious than gold and gives me a kiss on top of my head. I hug him and gently take the card in my hand.

'Take good care of it, Steve, and it'll take good care of ya. Remember that Steve. If times get hard for ya, get dis out and think about the Babe. He's special because he's such a good baseball player. He's special because he's a kind man. He neva does nothin' mean. He respects people."

"Grandpa Steve, do you think I'll be a baseball player?" I ask while puffing on my cigar and staring at the card.

"Steve, I don't know if goils will ever play baseball. What I can tell ya is ya can change ya name like the Babe did. Ya can be good at whatever ya do. Ya can be kind ta people and respect 'em. That's all ya ever have ta do, goilie."

I nod in agreement.

"Now let's go outside and rake leaves. We gotta get the stink blown off a' us so we don't get in trouble for smokin' cigars. Ya can wear my coat. I'll roll the sleeves up for ya. Put the Babe in the pocket so ya don't lose 'im."

We go up the basement steps with our rakes and an old pillowcase to hold the leaves. We are raking, talking and laughing. It's a little chilly, but sunny.

"I'll hold the pillow case and ya put the leaves in, Steve," says Grandpa.

I'm talking and picking up leaves.

He sniffs the air and makes a horrible face. "Ah, Jesus! What's that smell? Ya must a' picked up dog dirt. Ah, Jesus! Ya stepped in it too. Ya mudda's gonna kill us."

"Grandpa Steve. What do we do now?"

"Don't worry. Let's go down in the basement and clean ya up."

Lucky for me there's a washtub and some rags in the basement. Grandpa Steve pulls a little step stool over to the tub and puts my hands under the warm water. He soaps my hands.

"Steve, wash 'em three times. Give 'em the sniff test. If they still smell like a dog, wash 'em again."

He pulls off my shoes and scrubs them with soap and a brush. The smell is awful!

From upstairs we hear, "What are ya two doin' down there?"

"Little Steve was playin' in the coal bin and we're washin' her hands off in the wash tub," answers Grandpa Steve.

I'm sure that is the first time he has ever lied.

"Al," yells Grandma Steve, "don't soil her dress and make sure she doesn't touch her face. Do ya need Mae ta come down ta help?"

"Victoria, the two Steves are takin' care a' the situation."

I don't see the dog dirt on my sleeve and push my hair back with my cuff. I stink! Now I have dog dirt in my hair. Grandpa Steve is rubbing my shoes with a brush and the leather starts to look funny.

"Jesus! The two Steves are in trouble!" says Grandpa Steve.

"Al, are ya smokin' one a' ya cigars down there?" says Grandma Steve.

"We could use two cigars and a bottle of beer," Grandpa Steve says under his breath.

"No, Victoria . . . . just cleanin' Steve's hands."

"If ya don't come up right now, I'm sendin' Mae down there."

Grandpa Steve is hiding the rags and the scrub brush. My shoes are soaked. My long, blonde hair is dripping water in the front. My shirt cuffs are wet.

"Steve, lean over and let me put ya wet hair through the wringer a' the washin' machine. It'll get the water out really fast."

Hey, it's Grandpa Steve and I trust him. I lean over and he puts the ends of my wet hair in between the two wringers and he starts to turn the crank. The water comes towards my roots instead of the ends of my hair. He sees his error. I guess he's not used to doing the washing. I taste the soap and water pouring over my face. My eyes burn. I start to cry. Grandpa hits the release latch to the rollers, grabs me by the shoulders and pulls my hair out.

That's when Mom walks down the last step into the basement. "What's that awful smell? Albert Sauter! What are ya doin' ta Dee?"

At this instant Grandpa Steve throws a towel over my head.

"Me and Steve was just talkin' about the Babe, havin' a cigar and wishin' for a beer."

Mae and Yola At Yola's Wedding

Dee

Scare Me!

I'm not afraid of anything.

I mean nothing really scares me.

Well, maybe I get a little scared when the nuns talk about Purgatory.

You go there after you die and wait around.

I think it could be kind of lonely and dark. You don't know if you're going to heaven or hell—now that's scary. But I don't think about it very much.

I'm just a kid.

I don't know why, but I want to be scared now, really scared.

I'm not afraid to ask my Mom for things that I want. I ask again and again and when she gets tired of hearing me ask, she lets me get it, eat it, wear it or in this case, see it on the movie screen.

I want to see *The Mummy's Curse* starring Long Chaney.

"Mom . . . please . . . please. I promise I'll be good." I'm whining like the other kids I've seen at the Italian bakery who can't take no for an answer. "I want to see Long Chaney."

"First of all, it's Lon Chaney. He plays the mummy. It'll scare the hell out of ya and then y'll have bad dreams and wake up dead," says Mom.

"Aunt Yola says it's the best movie ever. Please, Mom, please . . . please."

"Since when do ya listen ta Aunt Yo? Why do ya want ta be scared? Why do ya want ta make a fool outta' ya self and scream in the movie theater? What if ya heart stops? What if ya face freezes? Use ya noodle, will ya?" says Mom as she pours a cup of coffee and lights a cigarette.

"Mom, look, I want to be scared by a movie," I plead.

"Wadda' ya crazy?" Mom asks. "Ya wanna be scared, look in the mirror."

"Mom, if you let me go see *The Mummy's Curse*, I promise to do all of the ironing for a week. I promise to go to bed on time. I promise to say extra Hail Mary's for Dad every morning and every night until he comes home from the war. Please . . . please."

"Extra Hail Mary's?" Mom lights a cigarette and blows a large smoke ring.

"I promise. Say I can. Mom, please! I can't explain it. I just want to be scared by a mummy."

"I don't know what ya taukin' about with the mummy thing, but if it'll help ya father, I'm all for it.

He'll be stateside in about six months. That's a lot a' Hail Mary's. Ya'll probably start sayin' 'em durin' the movie because y'll be so scared stiff," Mom says as she pours us a coffee with lots of cream. "If ya hear knockin', it'll be ya knees. And don't pass out or I'll have ta scrape ya off the seat and carry ya home."

"Thank you," I say hugging her. "You won't be sorry. I won't pass out."

"I have no idea where ya come up with ya crazy ideas. This one's a doozie," Mom says.

Aunt Yola walks into the room.

"Hey, Yo. What did ya tell the kid that makes her want ta go get scared by watchin' *The Mummy's Curse*?" asks Mom.

"Every kid I know is taukin' 'bout the movie. Kids love ta be scared. Look at you, Mae. Ya used ta ride on the back of a motorcycle. Ya were the only girl I ever heard a' ta do such a thing. Ya said ya did it because it scared ya," says Aunt Yola.

"Get outta' here! I did it because I had a crush on Johnny DeAmico. I got ta put my arms around him and whisper sweet nothin's in his ear," answers Mom.

"Yeah, and when he crashed the motorcycle and ya got glass in ya arm and hid it from Mom by wearin' a long-sleeved sweater in the summer, she kicked ya goolie when she found out. Ya got real scared then," laughs Aunt Yola.

"Uppa U.S., Yo! Why ya bringin' up my past in front a' my daughter?" Mom says raising her voice.

"Excuse me, but when . . . " I say trying to interrupt.

"I'm just pointin' out that ya liked ta be scared and do wild things, Mae," interrupts Aunt Yola.

"I'm wondering when I can go to the . . . " I say, trying to interrupt again.

"Dee, stop interruptin'. We're havin' a discussion here," Mom yells. "We're taukin' so put a lid on it!"

I put my hands over my ears and start singing in 'chicken opera' which sounds like, "bucka, bucka, bucka, bucka, buck ack, buck ack, buck ack, buck ack, buck ack!"

Mom and Aunt Yola stop yelling and start laughing.

"Ya can go ta work with me and Aunt Yola tomorrow 'n see the show. May God have mercy on ya soul." Mom slurps the last of her coffee and lights another cigarette.

We all take the subway from Corona to the Lowe's Theater. Mom kisses me goodbye after we put our coats in the office.

"The hours a' the night are few," she says in a scary voice meant to tease me.

"Can I have candy?" I ask.

"Ask ya Aunt Yola. Have fun, child a' the undead," says Mom.

I find Aunt Yola at the candy counter.

"Take what ya want, Dee", says Aunt Yola.

I take a chocolate bar.

"Jesus, Dee. Why don't ya live a little and have the new one with the peanuts?" she says, handing me her choice.

"Thank you, Aunt Yola."

She walks me into the theater and I sit in the back row. The newsreel is playing. A man with a nice voice is talking about the war and they show some big Navy ships and men in uniform. I think of my Dad and hope he is safe.

I unwrap my candy and settle down for a terrifying experience.

"Ugh! This is the worst candy I've ever tasted!"

I carefully wrap the candy bar wrapper back as close to the original packaging as possible. I leave my seat and peek around the doorway into the lobby. Aunt Yola is not by the candy counter. I walk to the counter, carefully place the partially eaten candy bar in alignment with those of its kind and take a plain chocolate bar. Mom would say I'm a kind-of-a-sewer of chocolate. I return to my seat.

Prompted by the image on the screen, guessing at what is written there; I say out loud: "Universal Pictures. Long Chaney. *The Mummy's Curse.*"

The movie goes like this. Dr. Halsey, from the Scripps Museum, has Princess Ananka in a box. She has been dead for three thousand years, but she doesn't even have one wrinkle or gray hair. Her old boyfriend is Kharis who was killed when she died because he stole the tana leaves for making a tea. The tea can bring her back to life. Kharis has already had a drink of the tea. It makes him mean and he kills people.

My Grandma Catherine is an herbalist and makes a lot of teas with herbs, but she never has trouble like Kharis. I wonder if she has tana leaves. They could come in handy if one of us dies. I'll ask her tonight.

I have to go to the bathroom, so I go as fast as I can. When I get back to the movie, there is some guy on a tractor in a swamp in Louisiana. The tractor is digging up mud. Here is the really, really scary part. Princess Ananka is in the swamp where there is no water, just mud. She's covered with it and she's alive. I don't know how she can see to walk, because her face and eyes are covered with mud. She walks to another part of the swamp where there is water and cleans herself off.

The only part that's truly terrifying is when the mummy's hand comes up out of the swamp. At first, I can't see the rest of his body, just his hand and arm which is covered in mud. Then I can see the rest of him and I'm so scared I can't move. It looks like he's going to reach out and grab me. I'd like to scream, but nothing comes out of my mouth.

Kharis can't talk either. His mouth and the rest of his body are covered with strips of cloth and he's full of mud. He walks with one arm straight out and the other one looks like he's doing the Pledge of Allegiance to the flag of the United States of America. If he has to go to the bathroom he's in trouble, especially if it's number two.

He walks to a place that looks like a church and sees Elzor, the bad guy. Elzor says to the mummy, "Drink from the brew of the nine tana leaves."

I make a mental note to tell Grandma she must have nine leaves or the tea won't work.

Right about now I look up and see Aunt Yola holding the candy bar I put back in the case. She grabs me by the arm and takes me into the lobby.

"I haven't been scared enough," I say.

"What's a matter with ya kid? Ya can't put a half-eaten candy bar back in the case. It ain't sanitary."

"I'm missing the Princess Ananka and the mummy," I answer.

"Whadda' ya taukin' about?" asks Aunt Yola.

Trying to wiggle out of her grip I say, "The candy tasted funny, like the peanuts were old, so I put it back."

We can hear customers coming into the lobby.

"Oh, get outta' here. We'll tauk later," says Aunt Yola.

As I walk back to my seat, Princess Ananka is saying, "Sometimes I think I'm two different people. I find myself in strange surroundings."

"Hey, I've had that feeling myself," I whisper under my breath.

Princess Ananka is now in a nice dress; she's clean, wearing makeup and looking through a microscope. She works for Dr. Halsey. She is studying the cloth the mummy is wrapped in.

I say out loud, "She has a job? She has been dead for three thousand years and she has a job?"

Aunt Yola comes in again to bother me. "We haven't finished the conversation about the candy bar young lady," she whispers.

I look on the screen and the mummy is carrying Princess Ananka up the stairs. He drags one leg and it makes him look scary. I'm worried that he may trip on Princess Ananka's white, silk skirt and fall down.

"They were old . . . the peanuts were old," I whisper.

"Well, that's no excuse. Candy bars cost money. I'll have ta pay for that one outta' my paycheck. Ya should have eaten it," her voice is getting louder.

I'm missing a really important part of the movie and I'm getting agitated.

"Look, I'm trying to watch this movie and get scared. If they had any brains, they would have put the brew of nine tana leaves in the candy and we wouldn't be talking about the candy bar with the peanuts that taste funny," I say loudly.

Aunt Yola stands there for a moment, mumbles something in Italian and walks away leaving me to experience terror until I get home to experience a different type of terror: answering to my Mom for my unforgivable, rude behavior.

Cousin Pat

Aunt Louise and Uncle Phil

The Dead Body

Cousin Patricia is nine months older than me.

My Uncle Phil married my Aunt Louise and Patricia is their blessed event.

She is my pain in the goolie on this one occasion.

Just because she's older, she thinks she's smarter. Well, I've got news for her. This may be the only time she comes close to winning a round of our ongoing emotional and mental wrestling match. I actually think I'm the victorious one since I maintain a shadow of a doubt when she tells me the story of the dead body. First of all, it's hard for me to believe someone like her who is dressed like a scarecrow.

Aunt Louise has no sense of fashion and an extreme dread of pneumonia. To guard against Patricia getting a chill and catching cold, she dresses her in five layers of clothing unless it's above eighty degrees. Then it's two layers.

In cold to cool weather, she wears two undershirts, one with a St. Christopher medal pinned to the shirt over her heart. On top of the undershirts are a blouse, a sweater and a jacket. She wears two pairs of pants over her white underwear.

Patricia looks three times her actual size until Aunt Louise begins to peel off the cotton and wool layers. As usual, Aunt Louise pinches my cheek as she yells, "Dee, I haven't seen you in ages!" She pinches harder and gives her grip a twist. She stops when Patricia starts to giggle. My cheek throbs for twenty minutes.

I hate it!

When Patricia is peeled like a banana from the layers of clothing, Aunt Louise goes into the kitchen for coffee with Mom.

Patricia says, "Dee, you'll have to go to kindergarten or you'll have no friends in first grade and feel stupid. I went to nursery school and kindergarten. Now, I'm in first grade and I know all of the answers and Sister Mary Catherine says I'm so smart I should be a nun."

I visualize Patricia in a habit with extra padding and a heavy crucifix dangling from her neck. Ha! How are you supposed to play basketball in a get-up like that?

"I bet I know something you don't know," whispers Patricia.

"So what? I bet I know plenty you don't know."

Stepping closer to me, she says, "It's something right under your very nose and you don't even know what it is. Go on, admit it. Admit that you don't know."

"OK. I don't know, but you know what? I don't want to know. I don't want to hear about it." I cover my ears and start to sing, "Toreador-o don't spit on the floor-o," my rendition of a Puccini opera.

Patricia is about two inches away from my nose with her face. Lowering her voice she says, "Shut up!"

Then with a poke of her index finger on my chest she says, "Why would you not want to know that there is a dead body buried in your yard?"

My eyelids start to flutter, "A dead body? Where? Who?"

Patricia grabs me by the wrist and pulls me under the stairwell. "Mom and I parked in the back by your garage and walked around the house. I saw the grave near the basement stairs. Let's make up some excuse to go outside, like we want to get some of that fresh air our Moms are always talking about. I'll show you the grave, if you aren't too scared."

"I'm not scared at all," I say feeling my knees shake and my palms sweat.

We walk into the kitchen. There is a cloud of cigarette smoke over the table. Mom and Aunt Louise are having coffee and Italian pastry.

"Aren't you girls having the best time!" purrs Aunt Louise. "It's so wonderful when cousins can get together. Mae, don't they get along so well?"

"They certainly do, yes indeed," says Mom blowing smoke out of the side of her mouth and spitting a small piece of tobacco onto her index finger.

"Can we go outside to get some *aira fresca* and play?" asks Patricia in a sweet tone. "We'll stay in the yard and not get dirty."

Dirt was a big deal to Aunt Louise. Patricia wasn't ever allowed to get dirty. It was considered unladylike.

"Of course you can go," Aunt Louise answers. "But only if Dee comes over to give me a hug and lets me pinch those cute, chubby cheeks."

I cringe thinking to myself, "This is a choice? Getting pinched so I can be shown a grave with a dead body in my own yard while Mom sits here drinking a cuppa' Joe?"

"Of course ya girls can go outside," Mom chimes in.

As I cling to my Mom and hug her, I feel that this may be the last time I feel the warmth of her body and the smell of her perfume. I am reasonably sure the dead body will come to life, rise up from the grave, grab me and pull me underground.

Aunt Louise changes her mind about pinching my cheek, and instead she reaches for the stack of jettisoned clothing and starts to pile it on Patricia. I put on one sweater.

We go out the front door and walk to the side of the house near the rose garden. I stop.

Patricia gets in front of my face.

"What's the matter? Scared? Scared of kindergarten? Scared of dead bodies?"

"No, I'm not scared. I'm just wondering if the murderer will be there, by the grave. What if he forgot something? What if he didn't cover the whole body? What if part of it is sticking out, like a hand? It happens in *The Mummy's Curse* with Lon Chaney. I saw it. I don't think we should go over there."

Patricia grabs me by the wrist and hauls me towards the basement door. "See, there it is. The grave . . . freshly dug . . . raked smooth."

I look. It is a grave: long and narrow with a smooth mound of dirt on top. My stomach feels tight. I feel like throwing up.

"Who do you think it is?" I can barely get the words out of my mouth. "Why is there a stick with a strip of white sheet tied to it stuck in the top of the grave? Is it a marker? A flag? The mummy has long rags wrapped around his body. There must be a body there, but whose body? Who's buried there?"

"Stop talking about a mummy and listen to me," she demands, looking around the yard to make sure no one's there.

"It's your gardener, Octavio," whispers Patricia, as she continues to keep a death grip on my arm. "It's not a mummy from some movie."

I gasp! "No! He was so nice! Who could do such a thing?" I have tears streaming down my cheeks. "We should make a cross and say prayers."

Patricia spins me around to face her and grabs both of my arms. "You should pray prayers of protection for yourself, sister. You could be next. The next time you see him, the next time he comes to your door, run and hide."

"Who . . . who?" By this time I have a really sick stomach.

"Tony, The Sack Man. That's who."

"The rag salesman? The one with the big sack full of rags on his back? The two-for-a-penny rags? NO!" I say, trying to hold back my flatulence.

"The very same. The one that knocks on your door every week trying to get Grandma to buy his rags. You know where he gets the rags? I'll tell ya. He tears up the clothes and sheets belonging to the dead people. Ask your Mom for a St. Christopher medal to wear around your neck for protection. Never take it off. I'm warning you."

I'm so scared and so sick to my stomach I'm sure I will vomit. I'm crying and sniffling. I'm trying to break free of Patricia's grip. I yell, "We've got to tell our Moms to call the police. They'll come. They'll ask questions. They'll find bad people who have done bad things. They'll be put in jail so the police can question them."

"You crazy? Grandpa is in the Mafia. No one in this family will ever call the police. Remember when Uncle Gene came home all beaten up and bloody? Nobody called the police. Remember when the money was missing? No police were called. Wake up and grow up. Wadda' ya doin', livin' in one of your plays?"

Holding my head to try to avoid an even bigger headache than the one I'm experiencing, I say, "Someone will miss Octavio when he doesn't come home. Someone will know something really bad happened to him."

Patricia grabs me again. "Only if YOU tell them. I'm glad I don't live here with the dead body. You're the one who'll have to go to bed at night knowing there is a dead body in your yard and the killer, Tony, is walkin' the streets."

Patricia notices rain clouds overhead. "Let's go in. I'm cold."

I stand motionless. "I'm worried about Octavio. He's under the ground over there and he's going to get wet."

"Come on. Let's go in and ask for a café latte and some cookies," bosses Patricia. "Nothing can be done for Octavio now."

"How can you eat? There's a dead man here!" I say wiping the tears from my face.

Patricia ignores me. "If our Moms ask what we were doing, let's tell them we were playing pretend school and we were nuns."

I feel horrible. We go inside and I head for the bathroom to wash my face and sit on the toilet. I hear Patricia telling Mom what a good time we had playing in the yard. "Aunt Mae, we're starving and so thirsty. May we please have a coffee and some cookies?"

"Yes, ya certainly may, but go and wash ya hands first."

I hear Patricia's footsteps approaching the bathroom door. Luckily, I'm at the hand washing stage because she opens the door without knocking.

"Move over!" she says, as she plunges her hands under the warm water, grabbing the soap from my hands. "Remember, not one word about the grave, the body, or the murderer."

We dry our hands and walk into the kitchen. I still feel sick to my stomach.

Mom places some cookies on Patricia's plate and pours a coffee for both of us. "*Mangia, bambinos, mangia. Prego.* Oh, ya girls are so cute! Louise, remember when life was so innocent and sweet?" asks Mom.

"Yes, the years go by so fast. They'll lose their innocence soon enough. One day you're holding them in your arms rocking them to sleep and the next day they're lovesick girls," Aunt Louise says, sweeping Patricia's hair out of her eyes.

Mom inhales a slow drag on her Lucky Strike cigarette. "Louise, let's hope they don't fall for some smooth taukin', tall, dark and handsome Italian," she says with a sidesplitting laugh.

"If they do, let's hope he's rich and will take care of his mother-in-law." Aunt Louise laughs and gives Patricia a pat on the head.

I sit at the table trying to act normal. Patricia glares at me. Mom says, "Dee, why don't ya do a song and dance for Aunt Louise and Cousin Patricia?"

Aunt Louise whispers, "I wouldn't encourage that, Mae. Remember when you went to Hollywood and came back a month later broke and with no job offers?"

"Oh, Dee will never be in the movies. She'll be a nurse or a teacher. She'll grow outta' the whole show business dream. For now, give us a rundown a ya latest play, Dee," says Mom taking a slow swig of caffeine.

I think to myself, *"Boy, do I have an idea! It's about a dead body buried in my yard and a murderer who comes to your door every week."*

"I'm working on a play about a soldier who goes to a foreign country and falls in love with a beautiful foreign woman." I make this up on the spot. Patricia looks at me and her jaw falls open in awe.

Aunt Louise says, "Oh, I don't know, honey. Men can't bring women back to the states. Can they, Mae?"

Mom shrugs her shoulders and lights another cigarette. "I don't think it would be fair ta their children."

Fair to the children . . . fair to the children? What about me? What's fair about not being able to tell the biggest secret of your life to anyone, even to your Mom? I'm getting really agitated.

Patricia drinks her coffee and eats about four cookies.

Mom laughs. "Bless her little stomach."

I stare at Patricia watching a purple color appearing under her eyes because of the sugar, but she keeps on eating. I have the same problem, and mom says I have a one cookie limit.

I have one cookie on my plate and I break it apart reciting part of the Holy Communion prayer. I hear Father Michael's voice in my head in Latin. Mom has told me this means, "This is my body given to you."

I would need more cookies than there are in the world for my sin of silence regarding the dead body. Miraculously, I get a few seconds of optimism.

What if Patricia was just trying to help me by giving me information?

(I doubt it.)

What if there isn't a body in that grave?

(Why would there be a grave and no body?)

What if Aunt Louise and Patricia had not come over to visit?

(I wouldn't have a headache and sick stomach.)

While I continue to try to reconstruct the entire scene like a badly written play that needs to be rewritten, I notice Aunt Louise is dressing Patricia in her many layers and it's time for our goodbyes. Patricia tries to hug me but she can't bend her arms because of the thickness of her clothing.

"I had a wonderful time, Dee. You are so much fun to play with. Thank you, Aunt Mae, for the delicious cookies and coffee," Patricia says while hugging Mom.

We all say our goodbyes, and finally, Aunt Louise and Patricia leave. Mom cleans the kitchen, and I go to the bathroom to be sick.

The next five days I have nightmares of a mummy's hand breaking through a muddy bog. I see images of poor Octavio clawing at the dirt as he takes his last breath. When awake, I check to make sure the front door is locked. It's the only rest I get from my fear; my guilt remains. Then it happens.

A knock comes at the door. Now I'm terrified. It's . . . it's . . . yes, Tony The Sackman with his big bag of rags. I'm frozen with fear. Grandma answers the door and greets Tony. I'm hiding behind her. She pulls me alongside her and we walk out onto the front porch.

Oh my God! He's showing her the white rags just like the one used as a grave marker on the end of the stick. I wriggle my hand out of Grandma's grip, take off to my right, and head for the side porch where I can hide until Tony either leaves or murders Grandma. I wonder if he murders more than one person a day. Does he murder kids too . . . kids my age? I've got to run, but my legs feel weak. I've got to get out of here.

Somewhere from inside my head comes a voice and I hear a pinwheel flutter. *Just take one step at a time and get to the side porch. When you get to the stairs, run into the yard and try to get in the back door. You can do it, Dee...you can do it...you have to do it.*

I'm panting. My mouth is dry. I look into the yard as I run down the porch stairs and into the back yard. I feel as if a monster is chasing me. I have to get away and save myself. Tears flood my eyes. I reach my trembling hands up to my face to wipe them away so I can see more clearly. If I trip and fall, Tony will catch me. I will die a horrible death.

Can you imagine my relief when I look into the garden? Guess who I see, planting roses on the mound of earth that Patricia convinced me was a grave? Octavio!

Mae

Welcome Home, Artie!

My Dad is coming home for a short visit after being away "at the war" for over a year. It's 1944. Even though he'll have to leave us again to go back to the war, Mom is excited to have time to visit Dad. Mom is acting silly, dancing around the house to the Ink Spots' recording on the RCA Victrola. We are listening to *If I Didn't Care.*

She whirls me around to the music while I stand on top of her slippers and then at the end of the music she does a dip just like Fred Astaire did with Ginger Rogers in *High Hat.*

"Let's see. What should I wear ta go pick up ya father?" She doesn't wait for an answer. She never listens to me with regards to fashion; I really know a lot about it from looking at her magazines and studying the clothing in the windows of the fancy 5th Avenue shops.

"I think I'll wear the blue crepe dress with the self-belt, brown, open-toed, snakeskin pumps and matchin' bag; and I'll wear the mink; oh, and a small hat. I put henna on my hair last night. Whadda' ya think a' the red?"

She doesn't wait for an answer. If she didn't really want a critique of the outfit, I doubt that she really wants to know what I think of the henna job. I'll be polite and not meddle. It's times like this I feel she still considers me a child.

Mom continues speaking non-stop, "Ya father will arrive at Grand Central Station at four o'clock. We'll be home by six o'clock. Get ya bath by five o'clock and put on the outfit I laid out. Remember, wear only what I put out for ya; none a' ya crazy outfits. Have Auntie help take ya rag curls out and put in the barrette so ya hair doesn't fall inta' ya eyes. Around six o'clock be lookin' out the vestibule window and y'll see us walkin' from the subway like two lovebirds."

I am thinking I've never seen birds walk down a sidewalk, but if that's what she feels like comparing her and Dad to, who am I to stop her?

Watching Mom get dressed, I think she looks the happiest I've ever seen her! I act as her assistant makeup artist. My job is to take the makeup out of the drawer of the vanity and line up everything in the order she uses it. I take my job as seriously as a surgical nurse. My Mom has a friend, Mary, who's a surgical nurse and she hardly ever laughs. Mom says that Mary is all business.

I'm all business too as I line up all of her makeup. There is a cream that smells like violets, luscious red lipstick, a tube of mascara with a small applicator brush, rouge, and Coty face powder. After putting on her makeup, she styles her hair in two pompadours that Aunt Yola refers to as "stronzos" (turds). *She Looks So Beautiful!* There is so much excitement and anticipation in the house. Even Grandma Catherine and Auntie Olympia get dressed up to greet Dad, who they call the returning hero . . . a hero other than Italy's dictator, Benito Mussolini, who receives monthly packages of silk shirts from my Auntie Olympia. They use few words in English, but they call Dad "Arta" which is as close as they can get to his real name, Arthur. "Arta" is the only man truly welcome in the house.

Grandma Catherine allows Grandpa to visit only on Sundays at dinnertime. She says that Grandpa will be *persona non grata* for this homecoming party because of his ties to the Mafia. Grandma Catherine gave Grandpa the *persona* name because she says being in the Mafia is a sin. He is never invited to special parties. No one asks Grandma Catherine to change her mind. She rules the household.

Aunt Yola has come over to help with the evening supper party preparations. She tells Mom, "Well, at least one a us has a date tonight. Have fun, Mae, but remember, Jesus and Mary are watchin'."

Mom rolls her eyes and they both have a good laugh. "Just wait 'til you're old enough, Dee."

"For what?" I ask as I hand Mom her pearls. "I'm not going to get old. I'm going to be like Bob Hope. In one of his movies he says he will always stay young."

"We don't know what ya taukin' about, Dee," says Mom as she puts on her fur coat and kisses me goodbye.

I follow her down the hall to the front door.

Screwing on her earrings, she runs out the front door laughing. "Always the comedian! Dee, you belong in front of a microphone. Tell ya Aunt Yola ta put out the good china and silver . . . and the best *vino. This* is a celebration!"

As I watch her run down the front steps, I realize all I know about my Dad is what my Mom has told me. He has been away so long I really don't know him. Mom says when they are together they rarely argue or get angry with each other. According to Mom, if they get close to being critical of each other Dad says, "Mae, ya slay me."

Then Mom says she answers, "Ya dirty dog!" She says they both laugh until tears shoot out of their eyes and she complains of her mascara running down her cheeks; one side of the tears being soaked up by her (ever present) Lucky Strike.

Mom says that Dad is funny just like Bob Hope, the actor and comedian. He has that twinkle in his eye and always loves to joke around. He turns many of her comments into jokes and she loves him for making her laugh.

Mom is always telling these stories to Aunt Yola and I'm a very good listener even though I'm a little kid.

Most of the time I don't get the jokes, but I love hearing about my Dad. Mom says he has a wonderful sense of humor and loves to tell stories.

It seems like it takes forever, but finally I hear Mom and Dad coming through the front door. The house explodes with screaming and everybody is crying happy tears. I'm hiding behind Auntie Olympia's big skirt and peeking around to get a glimpse of my Dad. He looks very tall, with blonde hair that's very short and he's wearing a Marine uniform. He looks just like he does in the picture beside my bed. Mom is wiping tears from her cheeks while Grandma Catherine and Aunt Yola are kissing Dad hello.

Mom sees me hiding and comes over and picks me up. Dad quickly walks over to me and grabs me from Mom's arms. It scares me, but I give him a big hug and he hugs me and says, "Oh, ya such a big 'un! What have they been feedin' ya? Ya growin' like a weed. It must be all a' that wine and spaghetti they been cookin' for ya."

Everybody starts laughing at me because I'm not saying one word. I just start to cry. I don't know what to say.

Mom says, "It must be a shock to see ya father afta' so long. Let's go sit down and eat some supper and visit. If ya don't feel like taukin', it's O.K., Dee."

We all walk into the kitchen and take our places at the table which is full of plates and plates of Italian food. Dad eats and eats! He must be very hungry. Maybe being a Marine means they don't get much food when they are at the war.

I'm not very interested in eating. I'm listening to everybody talking at once in English—except Auntie Olympia and Grandma Catherine. I guess their English isn't very good or maybe it's because, like me, they don't know what to say.

Finally, I get up my courage somewhere between the spaghetti, eggplant and chicken with red sauce. Just when plates are being handed back and forth in front of my face, I yell my first words to my Dad. "Dad, tell me a funny story about you and Mom!"

Everybody gets quiet, looks at me and then at Dad who's sitting opposite me.

Dad wipes the red sauce from his lips, takes a sip of wine and tells us a story that proves what a good storyteller he is and how much he loves Mom.

Dad tells it this way—the way it happened when Mom met him at Grand Central Station.

"Well, Dee, it was like this. We locked eyeballs as soon as I walked onta' the platform. We ran at each otha' like two high-speed trains. I picked up ya mother and whirled her around until the centrifugal force made her three inches talla' and I got as dizzy as a drunk swabby on a twenty-four hour pass. We did some 'belly rubbin' (kissing in a close embrace while dancing in a circle) and went at it 'hot and heavy' right there in Grand Central. Ya Mother was a sight for sore eyes, I'll tell ya.

"I said ta ya mother, let's go home right away so I can see how much Dee has grown. Well, we're walkin' on the sidewalk, hand in hand, and she steered me toward the subway.

"Mae, I hope ya brought the Ford. I haven't driven in so long I can't wait ta get behind the wheel.

"Ya mother stopped in her tracks and says, 'We don't have the Ford any more, Artie.'

"Wadda' ya mean, Mae? Where is it?

"At that point she grabs the lapels of her mink coat and says, 'I'm wearin' it!'

"I stopped for a moment with a big grin on my face and said, 'Ya don't say? And ya look damn good in it, Mae . . . damn good!'"

Dee

Haute Coiffure

Mom and Dad tell me they're going out to the Copa Cabana tonight to "raise a few (drinks) and dance 'til the sun comes up" to celebrate Dad's return to New York for a furlough which is like a very short vacation. They are going with Aunt Yola, her fiancé, Ike, and Lolly, who's a childhood friend of Mom's.

"Auntie Olympia and Grandma Catherine will both look after ya. Don't stay up too late," says Mom.

They gather at the house and all leave together to go get plastered (whatever that means). Grandma disappears to her room and this leaves me with Auntie who always goes to bed by eight o'clock after kneeling with her Rosary beads and saying her prayers like the good Catholic she is. Like the good kid that I am, I tuck myself in next to Auntie in the bed she had shipped over on the boat from Sicily. I need a step stool to climb up since I'm still a little tyke. As mom says, the mattress is so high I could get a nosebleed from the altitude.

As soon as Auntie falls asleep, which takes her all of two minutes, I sneak out of the bed like a runaway snake and head for the kitchen. I don't know exactly why, but I decide to cook.

I think I'll bake something. I get out the earthen mixing bowl that is very heavy for me to lift and put it on the table. I get out semolina wheat flour, olive oil, sugar, and salt from the pantry.

I open the icebox and remove eggs and cream. There is some left over plain spaghetti in there too. I take it out. I place the mixing utensils on the table along with all of the ingredients. I dump the flour into the bowl, not measuring. I add a few spoons of salt and two handfuls of sugar and stir the mass of confusion with a wooden spoon.

Stirring isn't easy, but when it's looking pretty good I add about a cup of olive oil, and crack open six eggs and throw them into the bowl. Now I've got a huge mess. It's thick and I think it definitely needs some cream. In goes a pint and I mix and mix.

Right about now I'm getting very tired. I feel weak and shaky, but I continue to improve my creation. I go get a bottle of perfume, pour it into the bowl, and add the cooked spaghetti.

I suddenly scoop out two big handfuls of the wretched mess and pile it on my hair. I add more and more until I have what was once in the bowl on my hair.

I am slathering it in dramatic shampoo swirls building a headdress worthy of Carmen Miranda, the wonderful singer and dancer who wears fruit on her head.

It smells pretty good and has a nice texture. I decide to leave it on as a hair conditioner. Mom puts olive oil on my hair from time to time for the same purpose.

The kitchen looks like some chef has gone mad, thrown a fit and used food as a weapon. There's flour, sugar and salt all over the kitchen table. I would like to clean up the olive oil I spilled, but it has turned to goo with some egg whites, sticking the dry ingredients to the tabletop.

Since I'm tired, I do what I think is sensible.

I leave it.

I climb back into bed utterly and completely exhausted. Auntie is deep asleep so I don't have to be careful about getting under the covers. I'm getting nauseated from the perfume and I'm freezing cold from having wet hair. I fall asleep.

The next thing I hear is the front door unlock. The party of five comes in whispering and giggling and then, like a faucet turning off, they are silent.

"What the hell is that smell?" Mom asks.

I hear them go into the kitchen. The women scream. The men gasp.

"Holy Jesus, Mary, and Joseph. What in the holy hell has happened?" Mom yells.

Now I hear her running for my bedroom. She flicks on the overhead light yelling, "Oh my God, she's white as a sheet. Auntie, wake up!" she yells in Italian. "What has happened ta Dee?"

Auntie always takes quite some time to wake up. She needs a cup of coffee to get her sensibility back from being wrapped in the arms of Morpheus according to Mom; only this time no coffee is being offered.

Auntie wakes up startled. She takes one look at me, screams and passes out. I figure it must be the spaghetti sticking out of my hair. Grandma enters the room to tend to Auntie just as Dad picks me up and carries me into the kitchen where he turns on the faucet, runs a sink full of water and plunges my head into it. He yells to bring a chair for me to stand on.

Ike, though stunned—this is the kind of family he's marrying into—brings a chair. Aunt Yola brings in some shampoo. Lolly is helping revive Auntie. Except for Dad and Ike, they are all Sicilian or Italian; yelling in Italian, cussing in Italian and everyone talking at the same time.

"What the hell do ya think ya doin'? Ya wasted all a' the food and now you're makin' yourself sick," Mom says in English as she helps wash my hair.

"Now, Mae, don't be so upset. Dee can explain. Can't ya, Dee?" says Dad hopefully.

I'm not ready to answer because I haven't made up a good excuse yet.

By this time they are complaining about how adding water to flour is not a smart idea because water plus flour equals paste. If they had only asked me how to remove the mess, I could have told them since I knew the recipe; but I let them go berserk, and laugh silently to myself. The show is wonderful; five adults in total chaos. I now have paste on my hair. The cooked spaghetti sticks out making me look like Medusa. Auntie, now revived, comes into the kitchen, sees me with pasta-tentacles sticking out of my hair, screams and passes out for the second time.

This time as she hits the floor only Lolly helps because I now have Grandma screaming over the others in a voice that sounds like orders to the Italian Calvary. Dad and Ike don't understand Italian. They ignore Grandma.

Finally, after six shampoos, I'm beginning to look like myself. Yola turns on the oven which is the only way to dry my hair unless I air dry. Ike puts a chair in front of the open oven door and all of them stand there waving towels at me. Dad says they all look like signal flaggers on a Naval destroyer.

Dad looks at me and says, "So, what made ya do this?"

Looking up at him I say, "I was thinking about what I wanted to be when I grow up and I thought I would want to be a chef like Francisco at Grandpa's restaurant; but then it was such hard work, this mixing and all, I decided it would be more fun to own a beauty parlor and do hair treatments on rich women."

They all stand there staring at me. Auntie and Grandma slowly back out of the kitchen. Ike leaves without saying goodbye. Yola runs after him. He's yelling that maybe a Jew shouldn't marry a Catholic after all. Dad, Mom, and Lolly start laughing so hard that I have to cover my ears and when I do I slowly withdraw a VERY long piece of spaghetti from somewhere in the midst of my shiny, blonde, beautiful hair knowing I have just won my first victory over my Dad. I didn't get in trouble and get punished.

Two days later Dad left for overseas.

As the months went by my memory of what he looked like and what his voice sounded like faded away until he was to me, again, a Marine in a photograph.

Grandparents' Sauter Home In Ridgewood,
Brooklyn, NY

Chickens?

My Grandma Steve is a good businesswoman. She is my Dad's mother, and Dad always says she has a really good head between her shoulders. He thinks I can learn a lot from her and, while I'm at it, I should hang around Grandpa Steve and learn how to tell a good joke. In other words, Mom and I are going to visit them in Brooklyn.

We have something in common. We all miss my Dad, overseas in the Marine Corps for these first five years of my life. Mom says Marines only get to come home for a short furlough, and she knows it must be hard to remember him, but he'll be home after the war is over. I have Dad's picture beside my bed and wish that he could live at home with us instead of being somewhere fighting a war. We think he'll be home for good in about three to six months. I hope so. I want to get to know him as a real person.

It will be good to go visit my Dad's parents and be in the house where he grew up and hear stories about what he was like when he was my age. Mom and I take the subway to Brooklyn, get off at the Flatbush station, and take a short walk to their house on 64th Place. It's the only house with big trees in the parkway. It's a wonderful, big, brown house at the end of the street. Grandma was born in this house, so it's very old. The train runs right beside the house. I love the sound of the train, even though it comes by every eight minutes.

The house is two stories, with a basement and a big lot next door with several different kinds of fruit trees. In back of the house are ten garages that Grandma leases. She charges ten dollars per month for customers to park their cars in there. We walk up the wooden stoop and knock on the leaded glass door. They are expecting us.

They both answer the door and we all yell, "Hello, Steve!" They hug and kiss me and tell me how much I've grown and compliment Mom on how pretty she looks.

Mom says, "Oh, thanks! Ya both look fit as a fiddle."

The house smells wonderful. There is an aroma of roast chicken coming from the oven as we walk down the hall towards the kitchen. Grandma Steve has also baked bread. She makes two different kinds of bread; one is a regular wheat loaf and the other is a dessert bread with dried fruit. I love them both.

"Whadda' ya know, Steve?" asks Grandpa Steve, as he pulls out a chair at the kitchen table. "Have a seat. Take a load off. Blow ya nose and clear ya head."

I laugh, sit down, and dangle my legs and feet. "I don't know much, Grandpa Steve. How about you?"

"Oh, I know so much ya could fill a book only nobody'd read it."

Mom and Grandma Steve are immediately busy in the kitchen mashing potatoes, putting butter on the carrots, and slicing the bread.

"So I hear y'll be movin' ta Camp Lejeune when ya Dad gets home. Wadda' ya think a' that?" asks Grandma Steve.

"Mom, where is that?" I ask.

"It's in North Carolina which is in the southern part a the United States. We'll live on the military base. Ya Father will be home with us at last. He has a feelin' that's where we're goin' even though he hasn't seen his orders."

"I'll have to go to school then," I say looking down into my lap, playing with the hem of my skirt.

"Yeah, ya had it easy all these years, kid," says Mom.

I really feel sad that I'll be leaving New York and my family and friends, but I don't want to start crying. Grandpa Steve realizes what I'm thinking and says, "Well, let's make hay while the sun shines!"

Into the kitchen walks their cat, Blackie. He is a very big boy. As usual, he walks over to me, makes one meow and scratches my leg.

"Ah, Jesus, I can't believe it!" says Grandpa Steve. "Ya must smell like a dead bird."

"You stop that, Al," yells Grandma Steve.

"Every time the kid comes over, it's the same thing. That damn cat! I'll get the iodine and a bandage," says Grandpa.

Mom comes over with a wet towel and wipes my leg. "Ya stackin' up these scratches like hash marks, kid."

Grandpa Steve puts the iodine on my leg and carefully wraps a bandage over my wound. The iodine stings, but I pretend it doesn't because I don't want Grandpa Steve to feel bad.

"Ya know, Steve, Blackie can open the Frigidaire, take out a bowl a' food, put it on the floor and eat it. I wish we could get 'im ta close the door. Ya grandmother is gettin' tired a' lookin' after his shenanigans and cleanin' up his dish."

"How can he open the door?" I ask wide-eyed.

Grandpa Steve points towards the sink. "Well, he stands back there by the sink, dat's about ten feet from the Frigidaire. He takes a run and jumps up against the handle, hits it with all fours and opens it. I tell ya that cat's got a lot a' fine qualities. I'm sure he's sorry fa' scratching ya. Whadda' ya say? Do ya forgive the rascal?"

"Sure, Grandpa Steve."

Mom and Grandma Steve have the table full of food. It looks and smells so good! I'm hungry and it's fun to get different food here. At my other grandmother's we eat Italian food every day.

"Grandma Steve? What kind of food is this?" I ask. "German Food?"

"No, this is American food—chicken, carrots, mashed potatoes and gravy. Tomorrow's a different story. Tomorrow we'll make sour fleish and cartuffel balls.

"How do you make that?" I ask.

Grandma Steve explains, "We soak a roast beef in vinegar water over night. That makes it tender. Tomorrow we boil potatoes and then press 'em through a sieve. Then we make balls like snowballs from the potato mixture and cook 'em in salted boilin' water while the roast is cookin' in the oven."

"I have never heard of that before. Cooked snowballs?"

Mom adds, "Ya Grandma Steve makes the best gravy ta go with it. Y'll love it! It's good ta try new things."

"Speakin' a' new things, after suppa', let's all go out in the back yard. I want ta show ya what I've done with the garages," says Grandma Steve.

I wonder what could be so interesting about ten garages holding ten cars that belong to other people. I pay attention to the conversation, so I don't miss anything.

Grandma Steve continues, "It was a big decision, but I gave it a lot a' thought. Since the war, many people have had ta sell their cars because they can't get tires or parts. After the Miller brothers told me they couldn't let from me any more, I began ta wonder what the future held. Then Mr. Kaufman told me he had ta sell his car and Mr. Eidleman the same. They all gave me notice that they no longa' needed ta let a garage. We were gettin' worried because our business was dwindlin'. Even though we still have the family livin' upstairs and payin' us monthly rent, we depend on that money from the garages. So one night, outta' the blue, I have this dream about Rhode Island Reds."

I'm listening to the conversation while making a big hole in the middle of my mashed potatoes. I top if off with a big chunk of butter and another spoonful of gravy lobbed into the crater. I wonder why Grandma Steve is dreaming about a baseball team—the Rhode Island Reds.

"I woke up Grandpa Steve in the middle of the night and said, 'Al, the future is chickens. Chickens lay eggs and that's cheap food. We got the garages and we'll turn 'em inta' coops. All we gotta do is take the interior walls down.'"

Grandpa Steve pipes up, "I says ta Grandma Steve, what about ol' Miss Berkholtzer's car?"

"Ah, Jesus," she says, "she hasn't taken it outta' the garage in two months. I'm not lettin' the spinster hold up my chicken and egg business. Everybody else has sold their cars."

We all laugh. They are very funny when they tell stories together or separately for that matter.

"So," Grandma Steve continues, "after suppa' we are showin' ya five hundred chickens."

I look at Mom and she is sitting with her fork in her hand and a shocked look on her face. I'll bet, like me, she has never seen a live chicken.

"Chickens?" Mom gasps. *"Five hundred chickens?"*

"Chickens is the future. Add some potatas' n' carrots and it's a meal fit fa' a king. Buy a dozen eggs and ya got cheap food fa' a week. I'll tell ya, Mae, we're chicken rich."

"Ya mean ya gonna . . ." Mom lowers her voice and asks, "kill 'em too?"

"Ah, Jesus, Mae, look what Mussolini has done ta ya country? We ain't so bad because we kill a few chickens," scolds Grandma Steve.

"I think I'll have another beer," says Mom. "Mind if I smoke?"

"Have ya beer while we do the dishes, Mae, n' then we'll go out back where ya can smoke, but not around the chickens. The coops are full a' straw," Grandma replies.

Grandpa Steve and I go into the living room and he shows me pictures of my Dad when he was young. He likes to tell me stories about all the trouble Dad got into with his friends.

"Ya father started smokin' when he was eight years ol'. He and Dutch would go unda' the bleachers at the ballgames and pick up butts. They'd take out the tobacco, pack it in a pipe, light it and share a smoke. Ya know boys do the damndist things that goils would never do."

He looks at me cautiously.

"Ya ever think about smokin'?"

"No. I only think about the cigars you give me that I pretend to smoke when we go down to the basement so you can smoke. Mom smokes a lot, but I don't like it and the smoke makes my eyes burn."

"Me thinks that women believe that smokin' makes 'em look sexy," says Grandpa Steve.

"What's sexy?" I ask.

"Ah, Jesus, Steve, I'm always puttin' my foot in my mouth. How 'bout a joke instead?"

"OK, Grandpa Steve. Tell me one that I can figure out."

"Two farmers meet on the road. They both have horses. The first one says, 'Morn'. That's short for good mornin'," explains Grandpa Steve.

"The second one says, 'Morn.'

"The first one says, 'What do ya give ya horse for the barts?'

"The second one says, 'Turpentine. Morn.'

"A week goes by and they pass each other on the road again. This time neither one has a horse.

"The first farmer says, 'Killed mine.'

"The second farmer says, 'Killed mine too. Morn.'"

I look at him wide-eyed. "I don't get it, Grandpa Steve."

"Ah, Jesus. Ya can't give turpentine ta a horse."

"Then why did he do it?"

"Well, it's a joke. Ya wanted me ta tell ya a joke."

"What good is a joke if I don't get it?" I ask.

"I can't help it if ya don't get it. Who's on first?"

"What?"

"No, what's on second. Who's on first?"

"Grandpa Steve!" I yell just as Mom and Grandma Steve come into the living room.

"Let's go look at chickens!" says Grandma Steve.

I run ahead towards the back door and Mom lags behind. She doesn't look very interested in going out to look at five hundred chickens.

We go out to the back yard and we notice a garden is growing.

"What's growin' here?" Mom asks.

"Carrots and potatoes—the full meal!" says Grandma Steve beaming.

Mom looks kinda sick like she does when she has too much food and wine, only she hasn't done that today.

Grandma Steve opens a door on the side of the garage and I follow her inside the coop. It's warm and smells a little bit like the pony ride area at Coney Island. There are light bulbs dangling from an electrical cord that is attached to the ceiling. The room glows with a soft light and feathers are floating in the air. Each chicken has her little house made out of a wooden crate. The crates are stacked on top of one another, two high. Some chickens are walking on the straw-covered garage floor.

I stand very still and soon six chickens walk toward me. I'm afraid they'll peck me. Mom, Grandma and Grandpa Steve are gathering eggs and not paying any attention to me. I'm not sure what to do, so I start to imitate the sound they make, 'cluck, cut, cluck, cut'.

I imitate what I see and hear in the movies, and I figure it would work in this situation. If I can sound like a chicken, they probably won't peck me. Clucking, they are all looking up at me and I am clucking back. They are all looking up at me and I'm clucking back to them. Then something strange happens. They start to look sleepy and lie down at my feet—six chickens!

Mom and Grandma see me in the middle of a circle of sleeping chickens and walk back from the other side of the coop.

"What on earth are ya doin', Dee?" asks Grandma.

"I'm talking to some chickens and calming them down," I reply.

"Well, that's a pretty good trick. We've had these chickens fa' two months and I've neva seen them so well behaved."

"Usually you have ta rub their foreheads or bellies ta calm them down, if ya can catch 'em," says Grandpa Steve, who arrives holding six eggs.

I step over two sleeping chickens and walk over to one of the crates where a chicken looks like she's sleeping.

"She's sittin' on an egg," explains Grandma Steve.

"Really? Can I see it?"

Grandma Steve gently picks up the chicken and sure enough, there's an egg in the nest underneath her belly.

"Are you going to sell this egg?" I ask.

"No, she leaves the ones that are fa' eatin' in her nest while she goes fa' a walk. If she thinks an egg will hatch a chick, she sits on it to keep it warm. This egg will hatch a baby chick," explains Grandma Steve.

My Mom is standing in the middle of the first coop with us. She looks a little out of place in her suit and high heels.

"Oh, Mom, can we have a baby chick?" I ask.

"No, honey. Not in Queens, only in Brooklyn," she says.

"Tell ya what," says Grandma Steve. "What if I save this one fa' ya? Ya can name it and when ya write me letters from North Carolina I'll let ya know how she's doin'?"

"Oh, thank you, Grandma and Grandpa Steve. This is one of the happiest days of my life. I never, ever had a chicken like this before. Only a dead one."

"Well, Lump," laughs Grandpa Steve. "We're gonna let this one die a' ol' age."

I look up at him and say, "Morn."

Grandpa Steve looks back with tears in his eyes. "Morn."

Mae (Pregnant With Dee), Art,
and Friend Rose

Arriverderci!

This morning instead of waking up at my Italian Grandma's house in Corona, New York, I'm waking up in the home of the German side of the family. I'm on the sofa in the front room of Grandma and Grandpa Steve's house in Brooklyn. It's a wonderful room with a big, dark blue sofa and two big chairs upholstered in the same nubby fabric and color. The furniture is so large I feel like Alice in Wonderland. There are heavy drapes of blue velvet on the front windows and a fireplace opposite the sofa. Three floor lamps are in the room, and Grandma Steve left one on for me last night so I wouldn't be scared.

I think it's nice when grown-ups do nice things for children, and Grandma and Grandpa Steve have always been so wonderful to me. I love them very much!

I'm lying in a bed Mom made for me on the sofa and there are two dining room chairs pushed against the sofa cushions to protect me from rolling out of bed and landing on the floor.

Last night I woke up several times hearing the sound of the subway train that runs on the elevated track beside the house. It passes by every eight minutes in the daytime, just like it is right now, but less often at night. I love the sound of the clack, clack, clack on the tracks. Whenever I hear the clacks, I count them and imagine that I am going on a trip to someplace far away like China where my Dad was stationed in 1938 long before I was born.

I guess it's a strange thing for a kid to do, but I'm thinking about my life, staring up at the ceiling and thinking about the differences in my two sets of grandparents. Mom's parents were born in Italy and Sicily. It must have been difficult to come to America on a big boat and not speak English, but with a lot of hard work they were able to earn money—Grandpa in the restaurant business and Grandma as a writer for the *Il Progresso* newspaper.

They bought their house in Corona and raised their family. They live in an area of the city where everyone speaks a different language and a little bit of English, and somehow they have managed to live without feeling different from the others in their neighborhood. Grandma Catherine tells me that we're one big *familia* and we need to get along with everyone, but I don't get it because she doesn't get along with Grandpa Canale because his friends aren't nice.

My Dad's parents were born in Pennsylvania and New York. At least they spoke English from the time they were kids, but as adults they still worked hard to get their house in Brooklyn and raise my Dad and Uncle Albert. Grandma Steve says they are 'resourceful'. She says a person in business has to supply what most people need—good, fresh food, selling eggs, chickens and vegetables. That's the way they get money to live on during these war years. Grandma Steve says when times are hard you have to use your noodle to get ahead. I don't know what noodles have to do with my head, but I guess it's some kind of joke. She and Grandpa Steve are always making jokes. They seem like regular, nice people and don't worry about too many things.

I'm different.

I was born two weeks before the attack on Pearl Harbor by the Japanese. My Mom says I'm a *War Baby*. I came to New York in 1944. I had lived in Portsmouth, Virginia where I was born in 1941 and in Quantico, Virginia in 1942 and 1943. Mom and I came to New York in 1944 because Dad was going overseas to Iwo Jima, Volcano Island, Japan.

I don't know any other children whose dads are in the military. When you get down to it, I don't know many children. That's why I talk and act like a grown-up. People say I'm poised for my age. Occasionally I see my two cousins, but not very often. It just feels strange to be around children.

I think life is different when a kid's dad isn't home for years at a time. I always try to remember my Dad, but I don't have too many memories of him. I really only know what he looks like because I look at his photographs or see him in a dream once in awhile. Once he came home on furlough, but I only saw him for a few hours and he went on vacation with Mom and left for the war again right after their trip. I guess I saw him when I was a baby, but I don't remember much of my life until I moved to New York.

Just recently, my Mom told me about where Dad had been before they got married in January 1941. My Dad joined the United States Marine Corps in December 1936 and was sent to Parris Island, South Carolina for training. From May, 1938 until September, 1940 he was in Shanghai, China. He came back to America and landed in the Norfolk Naval Yard in Portsmouth, Virginia December 1940. Then he met Mom, and I'm glad he did.

I have a good life here with my Mom, Grandmas, Grandpas, Aunts, and Mom's girlfriends. I don't know what it is like to have a Dad at home full-time like everyone else does. I guess that makes me different.

As I wiggle out of my bed, I think about how much my Mom has been talking about my Dad lately. She always reads parts of his letters out loud, so I know where he is and what he has been doing at the war. I think she worries about him a lot because we always light a candle for him when we go to church.

This morning when I walk into the kitchen for breakfast, Mom is talking about Dad to Grandma and Grandpa Steve.

"I've had my heart in my mouth for years," says Mom as I climb onto my kitchen chair. "I have lived in fear of gettin' a telegram," she says lowering her voice.

I look at Grandma Steve and she's wiping a tear from her cheek. I'm not sure what they are talking about, and I don't want to make them more sad by asking them to explain.

"The boys have a job ta do, Mae, and they do it well," says Grandpa Steve.

"The Marines are always the first ones ta land. They are tough and loyal," continues Grandpa.

"Well, look who has escaped the arms a' Morpheus," says Mom. "Did ya sleep well, Dee?"

"Yes, last night I dreamed I was on a train."

"I'll bet that made ya hungry. Were ya lookin' fa' the dinin' car?" Grandma asked laughing. "Let me make ya some eggs and coffee, Dee."

"That sounds good to me. Tell me more about the train that runs beside your house, Grandma Steve."

"Ya know, after a while the train becomes a part of ya life when ya hear it so often every day and night. I remember ya father paintin' the outside of the house and complainin' about how difficult a job it was. When he got ta the side a' the house opposite the train tracks, he'd have only five minutes ta paint and the other three minutes ta climb up or down the ladder. He couldn't be paintin' when the train came by."

"Why?" I ask.

"Well, some men in the last car with no manners would open the windows a' the train and make a wee-wee out the window and it would land on the side a' our house. A few times ya father was slow ta get off the ladder and he would get soaked," says Grandma.

"Oh, no!" Mom says, shocked by the story.

"Ah, it's just a little Holy Water. Nothin' a little soap and water wouldn't take care a', Mae," interrupts Grandpa Steve.

Grandma Steve gives Grandpa Steve the kind of look she gives when she is going to say that she's going to wash your mouth out with soap for saying something bad.

Grandpa Steve ignores her.

Grandma Steve serves me a cup of coffee, some bread with dried fruit in it and a fried egg. I stare at it thinking about wee-wee dripping down their house and wondering if it got on Dad's head.

"Arthur," says Grandma Steve, "was always good around the house. He loved carpentry and paintin'. He painted the baseboards every year from the age a' eight until he joined the Marines when he was eighteen. Mae, ya a lucky woman ta have such a helpful husband. I hope y'll always remember that."

"Oh, I know he was a good catch. I just want us ta be a real family and be together," answers Mom as she pours another cup of coffee. "I wonder what it feels like ta stay home and cook dinner fa' ya husband and daughter every night. He loves Italian food, so he'll be easy ta please."

"Mom," I ask, noticing the entire conversation is centering around my Dad, "tell me about how you and Dad met each other."

Everyone at the table turns their attention to Mom.

"Well, ya Dad had just gotten home from Shanghai, China."

"How did he get to America?" I ask wide-eyed with enthusiasm.

"He came by ship from China ta Portsmouth, Virginia. That's where Norfolk Naval Yard is," Mom continues as she sips her coffee.

"Then where did he go?"

"He came ta Brooklyn ta visit Grandma and Grandpa Steve. He was home on leave. I don't know if ya rememba, Dee, but afta' ya were born, he came home on leave before he left for Japan when ya were still very little. Leave is like a little vacation."

Mom continues as we all drink our coffee, "Ya Aunt Rose and I were out for a drink and he walked up ta us and introduced himself as Corporal Arthur Edwin Sauter. He was wearin' his uniform with a Good Conduct Medal, and a lot a' ribbons on his chest."

"What's a ribbon?" I ask taking a bite of bread.

"It's an award for bein' very good at somethin'. It's a small rectangle that a Marine puts on his uniform," Mom says drawing the shape on the tablecloth with her red fingernail.

"What did he do?"

"Well, let's see. He was so proud a' himself that he pointed ta each one and told us what he did ta earn them. He had several fa' Marksman awarded in 1937, 1938 and 1939. Some ribbons were for rifle marksmanship and some for pistol shooting. He was a Message Center Clerk, but also qualified ta be a Squad Leader in the Infantry.

"Jesus, Mae, I don't remember any a' dis' part a' the story," says Grandpa Steve. "Go on will ya? I wanna hear more."

"What's a *squad*?" I ask wolfing down my eggs and bread. "What's the *Infantry*? What's a *Marksman*?"

"Ya interruptin' the story, but I'll let ya get away with it this one time. A squad is a group a men. I don't remember how many. He was very good at leadin' the other men. The Infantry is made up a' soldiers, in this case Marines who fight wars on the ground. A Marksman is someone who can shoot a gun and hit a target, I think in the center, and it's called the bull's-eye."

"Oh," I reply, trying to take it all in, but not really understanding all of it.

Grandpa and Grandma Steve smile and look very proud.

"Well, as I was sayin', he looked very handsome and had a smile that would melt ice on a winter's day. Aunt Rose and I were both crazy about him. He had a wonderful sense a' humor."

"Then what happened? Tell me more!"

"I hope my son was polite, Mae," interjects Grandma Steve.

"Oh, yes, nothin' but a gentlemen. He offered us a cigarette, bought us a beer and asked each a' us ta dance. I thought he liked ya Aunt Rose because he asked her ta dance first."

"What kind of dance? Fast or slow?" I ask dreamily.

"Jesus, ya look like the lovesick girl in a Vermeer paintin'! Ya gettin' all my private information here!" laughs Mom.

I hold up both of my hands. "Yes, but I'm not holding a letter from my boyfriend like the girl in the painting."

Everyone laughs. We settle down and ask in unison, "Then what happened?"

"What is this? I got the Three Stooges here!" Mom giggles as she lights a cigarette.

I watch her blow a smoke ring as she holds the attention of the rest of us.

"Well, he walked us home ta Grandma Catherine's house. Aunt Rose always spent the night when we'd go out on the town."

"Was he *still* a gentlemen?" asks Grandma Steve.

"Yes, he was. He kissed both a' us on the cheek, and asked us ta go out with him the next night."

By this time, I'm really getting excited to hear the rest of the story.

"Mom, hurry up. Tell us the rest of the story," I plead.

"Well, we did this several nights in a row. The last night he told us he was goin' ta return ta duty for some maneuvers or somethin'. He walked us home, kissed both a' us good night, turned around as if ta walk away and then spun around on his heels ta face us again yelling, "Catch!"

"Catch what?" I ask.

"*Aspetta*! Wait. Let me finish," instructs Mom holding up her hand to silence me.

Mom continues, "As he yelled 'catch', he threw a small box toward me. I thought it was for Aunt Rose, but it was like a curve ball and it came ta me. I caught it with both hands. He had this big smile on his face. I opened the box and inside was a diamond engagement ring! I tell ya, I was floored! I stood there in shock for a moment. Aunt Rose started screamin', 'Oh my God, Mae, oh my God!'

By this time we are all leaning with our elbows on the table and our chins resting in the palms of our hands staring at Mom. Grandma and Grandpa Steve have tears in their eyes and their mouths are hanging open.

"Then Artie said, 'I need an answer tomorra' night, Mae. I'm goin' ta be shipped out soon ta Baltimore, Maryland.'

"He walked off with that big grin, lookin' over his shoulder. Ya Aunt Rose and I were up 'til dawn taukin' about what I should do. I loved him like crazy and I intended to say yes."

Grandpa Steve says laughing, "Well, Arthur is a chip off a' the ol' block. I would a' done the same thing. Give us the coup the grassy, Mae."

Controlling the moment, Mom takes a long drag from her cigarette and finally lets the smoke out of her mouth and it floats over the table like a big cloud.

"The next night Artie picked me up in front a' my house in Corona. I had ta lie ta my Mother about goin' out because by that time she was gettin' suspicious. I told her I was goin' ta stay late at Aunt Rose's house."

"You lied!" I scold.

"Well, if I didn't lie, ya wouldn't have been born. So there!" Mom says hugging me.

"Anyway," she continues, "Artie acted like nothin' special was goin' on. We went ta the bar for a beer and he got me on the dance floor—huggin' and dancin'. I couldn't resist. I couldn't wait ta tell him yes. So I did. We were so happy! Artie had a big grin on his face.

"We were married three weeks later, January 25, 1941 in the residence a' J.C. Spence. I'll neva forget the address--712 West Main Street in Elizabeth City, North Carolina by a Justice of The Peace, Mr. Louis."

"I rememba gettin' the telegram," says Grandma Steve. "The following week ya father brought ya mother here ta visit. We thought he made a wonderful choice."

Grandpa Steve nods in agreement.

Mom continues, "I wish my Mother had been so easy ta please. She was really upset according ta my sister, Yola. Even though she didn't attend Catholic Mass every day, she followed the laws a' the church.

Apparently she told Yola that since we were both marryin' non-Catholics, we would be immediately excommunicated from the church."

Grandma Steve looks worried. "It sounds serious, Mae. Can it be fixed?"

I look at everyone at the table. I don't know what excommunicated means, but it must be bad.

Mom gets some tears in her eyes, but they don't drip down her cheeks.

"I feel that I have made my choice. I still believe in God, but I'm not so sure I believe in my Mother. I think parents should be more lenient with such matters. She always said everyone was one big family and then she treated me as if I was an outsida'. It was 1940 when we met. Not the Dark Ages."

Grandma leans towards Mom and hugs her.

"Let me make a fresh pot a' coffee, Mae," Grandma says softly.

Mom continues, "My Mother was even angrier with my Sister, Yola. She married a Jew."

Grandpa Steve quickly says, "Now that's gotta be worse than a Lutheran!"

Grandma Steve shoots another look at Grandpa Steve that always goes along with the I'm-going-to-wash-your-mouth-out-with-soap promise. She never actually washes anyone's mouth out with soap, but hearing her say it usually gets the person to apologize.

He doesn't.

"Al, that's not a good example fa' Dee."

By this time Mom is crying.

I've never heard my Mom talk about this Catholic thing before, so I don't know what to say. I used to go to Catholic Mass every day and now I know why Mom always said it was a secret. I remember her telling me that one day we would move out of New York and I wouldn't be able to go to Mass anymore and I couldn't tell my Dad that I had been going either. I guess I'm going to be the excommunicated word too and that makes me an outsider instead of a member of one big *familia*. The only *familia* I'm in now is with Mom and Aunt Yola—the three "ex" girls—that's us.

Mom is having a fresh cup of coffee and she has stopped crying. I think the serious conversation is finished. I've eaten all of my breakfast and ask to be excused so that I can get dressed.

"Of course, Dee," Mom answers.

Grandpa Steve asks, "Want ta go feed and water the chickens, Steve? This is a special day and we ought ta be happy. Besides, ya Mom and Grandma are goin' ta do a lot a' cookin' today. It's sour meat and potato balls fa' dinner," says Grandpa.

"Oh, Mom, can I?"

"Sure, kid, but rememba, ya can't take a chicken home ta Corona."

"I know. They don't have chickens in the back yards there."

I climb down from my chair and go into the bathroom where I brush my teeth with tooth powder, wash my face with a wonderful smelling soap and put on my clothes. The outfit is new. I bring my hairbrush to the kitchen so Mom can fix my hair.

"Mom, I love my dress!"

"Oh, ya found the surprise. Ya look very grown up! Don't get chicken feathers on ya outfit. I want ya ta stay neat and clean until dinner."

Grandpa responds, "Don't worry, Mae. I'll see that she returns clean as a whistle."

Grandpa Steve and I go to the backyard and I hold the pan of seed he gives me and start throwing seed on the ground by the small door that allows the chickens to come and go from what used to be the garages. About twenty chickens come out for the seed. This is my favorite job at Grandma and Grandpa Steve's house. I'm saying, "cluck, cut, cluck, cut" and the chickens are talking back to me. Grandpa is pouring water into their water trough.

Grandpa Steve says, "Let's take a rest and smoke a cigar and eat some licorice."

"Oh, that sounds good to me. Feeding chickens is hard work," I say putting the seed pan on the ground and watching several more chickens head for the pan.

We sit on some big rocks in the side vegetable garden. We both hold a cigar, but Grandpa lights his. I wear the band on my finger and just hold my cigar.

"Well, Lump," says Grandpa Steve. "I think y'll be goin' back ta Corona tomorrow ta stay at Grandma Canale's house. I'm gonna miss ya, kid."

"Oh, I can come another day, Grandpa Steve."

Grandpa's eyes get watery.

"Sure, kid, sure. We'll see ya soon. Hey, ya wanna play Jacks?"

"I'm gonna win ya," I say teasing Grandpa Steve.

We are in the yard a long time playing Jacks and watching the chickens. Then Grandpa Steve says, "Ya know, Steve. Maybe it's time ta go inside. Let's take a look at my pocket watch. What time does it say?"

I look carefully at the watch.

"Eleven and a half," I calculate.

"Dat's eleven thirty. Da six makes it thirty," explains Grandpa Steve.

"Let's go in the back door and surprise the troops in da kitchen."

We walk into the kitchen and it smells like roast beef cooking and other wonderful smells like bread and cabbage. Mom and Grandma Steve are all dressed up, but wearing aprons and if Mom had any sadness from the "ex" conversation, it's all gone now.

"Go in the bathroom and wash ya hands, Dee," says Mom.

Just when I'm walking into the kitchen, there's a knock on the door.

Everyone looks at me.

Mom says, "Oh, let's see who it is."

We all walk to the vestibule.

Grandma Steve says, "Open the door please, Mae."

Standing in the doorway is the most wonderful sight I have ever seen, but for an instant, I'm not sure who it is. It's a Marine in uniform with lots of medals and ribbons on his chest. He looks like all of the pictures I've seen of my Dad. I am so surprised that I feel frozen. I don't move or say anything.

My Mom yells, "Artie! You're home!"

Mom, Grandma Steve and Grandpa Steve all hug and kiss him at the same time. Everyone is crying and screaming.

I feel kind of numb.

The Marine drops his big bag on the porch and hugs Grandpa Steve.

"My boy, ya a sight fa' sore eyes," says Grandpa Steve.

"Have they been feedin' ya?" says Grandma Steve.

Mom has her arms wrapped around Dad's neck and he's picking her up in the air and spinning her around kissing her at the same time.

"Ya home! Ya home at last!" screams Mom.

All at once, they realize I'm standing behind them stunned.

Mom crouches down beside me and says, "Dee, meet ya Dad!"

Dad picks me up and kisses me on the cheek. "Oh, ya such a big girl! Whadda' ya know? How ya been?"

I'm so surprised that I don't know exactly what to say. Everyone is looking at me, waiting for me to say something.

"I have a black tongue," I say, still in my shocked state.

"What?" Mom, Dad and Grandma yell simultaneously.

I stick out my tongue and sure enough, it must be black because everyone looks shocked except Grandpa Steve.

"Ah, Jesus! Me and Steve have been smokin' cigars and eatin' licorice again. Well, that's one fa' the books; a black tongue!"

Grandpa continues, "Dee, if anyone ever asks ya what the first thing was ya said ta ya Dad after not seein' him for most a' ya childhood, ya can tell 'em this story."

We all laugh and walk into the kitchen. For the first time in my life, I remember sitting down to dinner with my Dad present at the table. I realize that he is home for good.

Arthur Sauter, USMC

The Jacket

I can't remember what my Dad actually looked like in person. Mom says war changes people, but I don't know if she means my memory or my Dad's looks. I remember Mom being excited years ago when she went to Grand Central Station to meet him and there was a family dinner to celebrate his return to New York, but he only stayed for a couple of days and then went on vacation with my Mom. The day they got back, Dad left again to go to Japan. I was very little, but I remember he kissed me on the forehead, and said he was going away so that Americans would be safe and free, but I didn't know what he was talking about.

Today is different. It's his *real* homecoming.

I was so surprised that I almost fainted when my Mom opened the door here at Grandma and Grandpa

Steve's house in Brooklyn. At first, I didn't realize that the Marine was my Dad. It took a few seconds for my brain to understand that it was really him. He looked very handsome in his Marine Corps uniform and he was even wearing his hat. A big, heavy bag fell with a loud bang on the porch when Mom opened the door.

When Dad picked me up to kiss me hello, he smelled like Autumn leaves when they're wet and you decide to rake them and light a fire like when Grandpa Steve and I work in the yard.

It's funny to say this, but to me my Dad was a picture in sepia rather than a real, flesh and blood person. It was kind of like having a paper doll—flat and small. To see Dad in the doorway life-size was a jolt. Mr. Katz, our butcher, once told me that lightning struck his house and it sent a jolt of energy through his body. Well, that's how I felt seeing my Dad standing in front of me. It was a thrill and a shock at the same time. He was a life-size, moving, talking, real person.

As we all walk from the front door into the kitchen, Mom says, "Dee, ya father's goin' ta be home for many years and we're finally goin' ta be together as a family."

Grandma Steve chimes in, "Oh, after all these years ta see each other every day will be a wonderful thing."

I have a problem. I don't really know my Dad. I guess the best thing to do is be quiet and watch him and see if I can figure out what kind of man he is. One thing I can tell already is that he smiles a lot, talks like

Brooklyn people talk, and likes to smoke cigarettes like Mom does. His hair is the color of honey, just like mine, but it's very short and wavy. His eyes are not like my green ones—they're blue.

We are all in the kitchen. Grandma Steve makes Dad eggs, bread, coffee and pours him a glass of milk. The four of us sit at the kitchen table staring at my Dad eating and everyone is talking at once except me.

I don't know what to say.

"I tell ya," Dad says wiping yolk off his lips. "I have been dreamin' a' my first meal at home when I wouldn't have ta worry about leavin' again in a few days."

"Ma, all we had to eat was our K-rations. They were awful. On our way back stateside, the seas were so choppy on board ship nobody felt like eatin'."

"We're just so happy that ya finally home. We'll make ya anything ya want; steak, chicken, sauer fleisch and kartoffel balls," Grandma announces.

"Sour meat and potato balls?" Dad yells. "I'm in Heaven! When are ya makin' that? Are we goin' ta have red cabbage too? I haven't had German food in years, Ma. Oh, this is gonna be good!"

Mom is rubbing Dad's shoulder with her hand and smiling into his eyes. She says in a dreamy voice, "We started yesterday and by this afternoon the meal'll be ready. It'll be a real feast for ya. Of course, for good luck there'll be pickled herring too."

I have never eaten this stuff so I don't know what they are talking about. I smell the meat roasting in the oven; it smells a little bit like vinegar. I feel like I'm watching a movie. Dad looks at me and smiles like I'm sitting in the audience.

Grandpa Steve says, "Art, ya better be in on the latest change in the family. Dee has changed her name ta Steve and renamed ya mother and me Steve too. We're all Steve. Mae has kept her real name. Do ya need a score card ta keep the players straight?"

"No, Pop. Mae wrote me a letter explainin' that ya and Dee had a tauk and ya told her that she could do almost anything she wanted ta do with her life and she made the choice ta change her name, as well as yours. Folks have ta have a mind a' their own. I think it's a fine idea as long as it's fine with Mae. We neva use the name on the birth certificate anyway. We always call her Dee, but my favorite name is Marielaina. We put that name and others in a hat and pulled two names out and that was the name we picked the day she was born. If Dee wants ta be Steve, then Steve it is," says Dad glancing at Mom.

"God knows I always followed my own heart, Artie. This kid is a real doozie. She has crazy ideas sometimes. She wants ta be an actress and write plays for Hollywood movies. Sometimes she draws costumes while she's singin'. She lives in her own dream world. She has wild notions," explains Mom as she lights Dad's cigarette.

I scoot down in my chair trying to hide and I'm thinking I'm glad I didn't get stuck with the names they wanted to give me.

"Now, Mae," Grandpa Steve interrupts," Dee's not like other kids. She's very grown up fa' her age. She tauks like a grown-up, does chores without bein' asked and can figure things out as good as any politician. I'm sure she'll have no trouble gettin' through life."

Scooting down in my chair has worked. They are talking about me as if I'm in the other room. I'm glad because I don't know what to say to join the conversation. I'm learning a lot about what they think of me, but I don't think I'm as smart as President Harry Truman.

Grandpa Steve changes the subject as I feel my hot face cool off.

"So, wadda' ya think a' bein' back in the good ol' U. S. of A., Art?"

Dad loses the grin on his face as he looks down at the table. "It was pretty rough. I saw Mainland China in 1936 and '37. It was a beautiful place before the war. The amount of destruction war creates is somethin' I'll neva forget."

Mom squeezes Dad's hand. Grandma, with tears in her eyes, pats Dad on the shoulder and says, "At least God has returned ya home safe and sound."

"Ya know, Ma, it's hard ta believe that there's a God who allows war ta happen. Sometimes I wonda' if there really is a God," Dad says shaking his head and taking a long drag from his cigarette.

Everyone at the table is quiet. Maybe we shouldn't have changed the subject in the first place.

Mom looks very sad. "Ya know, Artie, sometimes when I hear sad stories, I wonda' about God too, but I always come back ta the fact that there's a lot a' good things; ya know, blessings. For instance, we have a daughter, a nice family, a roof ova' our heads, and plenty a' food which I think we should start fixin' for our celebration dinner. I'm thankful ya home."

Everybody smiles and wipes away tears from their cheeks while I just sit and try to figure out something to say that would make sense.

"Hey, Dad. Do you want to see the chickens?" I ask.

Dad is looking at his coffee cup and spinning it around on the saucer.

Grandpa Steve breaks the silence, "Now that's a good i-dear. Nothin' like some chickens ta cheer up a guy and we need ta feed and water 'em anyway."

Dad looks like he's back from a bad dream. "Let's go see the chickens!" he says. "How many ya got? A coupla' dozen?"

Grandpa winks at me, like we have a secret about the number of chickens.

Mom and Grandma stay in the kitchen to make the potato balls and to talk about girl stuff. I want to be with 'the boys'. That's what Grandpa Steve calls the three of us.

Us boys walk out the back door and past the vegetable garden toward the garages. Grandpa Steve points, "They're in there, Art."

"Pop, this was a good idea; turnin' the garages inta' coops," says Dad as we walk through the small garage door into a cloud of white feathers and clucking.

The chickens must be happy to see Dad. I am really surprised that he can speak chicken like I can.

Dad calls out, "Cluck, cut, cluck, cut! There are hundreds of 'em!"

I stand beside "the boys" and soon we are surrounded by a hundred or so chickens. Some are flapping their wings and trying to fly and some are prancing around like the drum majors in a parade on the 4th of July. Dad sits right down on the feathered-covered floor of what used to be the garage and the chickens come right over to him. He reaches into his pocket and pulls out a piece of bread and they all go wild clucking and flapping.

"Sit down. Take a load off," Dad says to Grandpa and me.

"They'll peck me," I say with a quiver in my voice because I'm terrified of so many chickens. Sitting down will make it hard to run away, if I have to.

"Na. They won't peck ya. Sit here between Grandpa and me," says Dad. "Ya know, they're just taukin' to ya."

It was a sight: the three of us sitting right in the middle of so many chickens and Dad holding out little bits of bread. At one point there are chickens in his lap and a chicken on his shoulder. We all laugh because I scream whenever a chicken flies in front of us, but I feel safe because "the boys" have everything under control.

There are so many white feathers floating through the air it reminds me of a snowstorm. While Dad and Grandpa Steve are talking to chickens, I think about collecting a bunch of the feathers to make costumes for a play I'm going to write someday about an angel. I think, after dinner, I'll see if Dad might collect feathers with me, but I'll have to get some courage to ask him.

We sit with the chickens for a long time until Grandpa wants a cigar, Dad wants a drink, and I need to wash my hands. I smell like chickens.

"Let's go back ta the house and see the women-folk," says Grandpa Steve.

Dad, throwing his arm around Grandpa Steve's shoulder says, "If we know what's good for us, we'd better call 'em chefs."

"Ah, Jesus, Art, let's not let ya ol' man get inta' trouble. I'll neva hear the end a' it. I stand corrected, son."

Dad laughs.

We walk through the back door and go our separate ways. I go into the bathroom, climb onto the step stool Grandpa Steve made me and wash my hands. I have to pick feathers out of my hair and they are so pretty I decide to stick them on the front of my sweater.

I can hear everybody talking in the kitchen, but it's muffled like when you can't hear the radio very well because you're in another room.

I finish decorating my sweater and go into the kitchen.

"Whadda' ya doin', Dee? Ya look like ya were hit by a blevey," yells Mom.

"What's that?" I ask.

"It's many things, but in this case it's an explosion in a mattress factory," Mom says.

We all have a good laugh.

Grandpa Steve says, "Well, I'm goin' ta go have a cigar in the basement and put some coal in the furnace."

Grandma Steve is busy making bread. "We'll be a while cookin', Mae and I," says Grandma Steve.

Dad looks at me. "Dee, wanna help me unpack my seabag?"

"Yes. Want to help me pick up feathers later, Dad?"

"Yeah. Are ya makin' a mattress?" Dad says as he picks me up and carries me through the dining room and into the hallway where he dropped his seabag just inside the vestibule.

"Let's hang this stuff up and make a stack a' laundry. I can show ya some medals and ribbons."

He opens the big, green bag and lifts out underwear, uniforms, a pair of field boots, a pouch containing a toothbrush, toothpaste and soap, and some letters from Mom.

"This stuff has been halfway around the world and back again. Here, ya hold the coat hangers and hand 'em ta me when I need 'em."

"What's this?" Dad says, pulling out a chocolate bar.

I feel my eyes get big and my smile get bigger.

"Let's have some chocolate, just the two a' us," Dad whispers.

"Yum. Better than a cigar!" I giggle.

Dad unwraps the chocolate bar and we enjoy the taste even though it's very hard to break it into pieces. As we eat our chocolate, he reaches into the seabag again.

"This is my jacket," says Dad as he holds a folder full of papers.

I look puzzled. "My jacket looks like a coat."

"This jacket is a folder that holds all a' my Marine Corps papers. Here, I'll show ya. Let's sit on the floor."

We sit down next to each other. Dad opens the jacket.

It isn't put together like a book. It has a metal clip on the top that holds the pages so they don't fall out.

He picks up the top page. "This letter made me a man. It changed my life. I'll read it ta ya."

United States Marine Corps
Eastern Recruiting Division
Headquarters, District of New York
Federal Building, Washington & Christopher
Streets
New York, N.Y.

3 December 1936

Mr. Arthur E. Sauter
67-02—64th Place
Ridgewood, N.Y.

Dear Sir:

> *If you will appear at this office on or before Tuesday, December 8th, with the enclosed consent form signed by your parents in the presence of a Notary Public, we will be able to make arrangements for your enlistment and transfer to the Marine Barracks, Parris Island, South Carolina, during the month of December, provided you still are able to pass the required physical examination. In the event that you do not wish to enlist in the Marine Corps at this time please advise us, by return mail, using the enclosed self-addressed envelope which requires no postage for your reply, in order that we may fill your vacancy from among others on our waiting list.*
>
> *Very truly yours,*
> *A. E. Simon,*
> *Major, U.S. Marine Corps,*
> *Officer in Charge.*

"I enlisted 12 December 1936," Dad says looking at the letter.

"What's enlisted?" I ask.

"I signed on ta be a Marine for four years. I was eighteen years old. The Marine Corps trained me ta be a man. Ya know what U.S.M.C. stands for?" Dad asks looking at me.

"I don't know the answer," I say looking into my lap. I hope he isn't too disappointed in me.

"It stands for *Useless Sons Made Comfortable.* It's a joke. If there's one thing ya ain't in the military, it's comfortable. We worked hard shootin' rifles, crawlin' on our bellies and up cargo nets. We were drilled mornin', afternoon and night."

"What's drilled? What's a cargo net?" I ask enthusiastically.

"Ya gotta lot ta learn, kid. This could take awhile. Drilled means trained and a cargo net hangs over a ship or on an LST and ya climb up or down the net ta get in or outta' the boat."

"Oh," I answer, but I never heard of this before and I'm not really sure what Dad means.

"Anyway, it says here on my Discharge Paper that I had a tour a' duty in Shanghai, China from '38 to '40. Here's a list a' my medals and my weapons qualifications. I was a sharpshooter. When I got back stateside I was a Corporal. The Marine Corps gave me $42.00 a month and $23.60 travel allowance from Portsmouth, Virginia back home ta Brooklyn. That's when I met ya Mother. We got married and a year later ya were born."

Dad turns to the next page and looks at me. "I think ya should know where I've been, Dee. It's gotta be strange for a kid ta know she has a father, but hardly sees him for years. I owe it ta ya ta explain what I been doin'. Even if ya don't understand it now, maybe someday y'll see these papers and remember that we had this here conversation."

Dad continues, "This page says I re-enlisted on Christmas Eve a' '40 'til 23 December '44. I was in the thick 'a things from Christmas Eve a' '44 to '46."

Dad looks at the page. His face is serious, like he's thinking. He reads out loud:

> "Battles, engagements, skirmishes, expeditions: *Participated in the assault and capture of Iwo Jima, Volcano Islands from 19Feb45 to 27Mar45; Participated in the occupation of Kyushu, Japan from 22Sep45 to 15June46; Participated in Atlantic Fleet Landing Exercises in the Caribbean Area from 8Feb47 to 22Mar47..* Wounds received in service: *None*"

"I was a lucky one, not gettin' wounded."

Dad continues, "When ya were a baby I was in First Sergeant's School in Quantico, Virginia. I studied hard. In '42 I was an instructor in drills, infantry, weapons and tactics. I used everything I learned in school ta take care a' myself overseas. Here's a Battalion List a' the men who were wounded or killed. There are pages of 'em. I was the one who typed these lists a' names."

Dad is talking to me, but he seems to be far away. I see tears in his eyes, but he's not crying. He stays quiet for a while, then he continues, "There were so many that were killed. . . ." Dad's voice gets very quiet.

I want to ask him a question, but I'm not supposed to talk about anything that has to do with Catholic Mass because he's Lutheran. Mom has allowed me to be raised Catholic like her side of the family, but this is a secret she is keeping from Dad. I can't stand to see him looking so sad. I could get in a lot of trouble if Mom finds out what I'm about to ask.

"Dad?" I say softly. "Did you ever see an angel standing next to you?"

Dad looks at me like I'm crazy.

"An angel? No, I ain't neva seen such a thing! Well, maybe in a picture, but not for real." He's staring at me. "Wadda' ya mean?"

I look at him wide-eyed. I am remembering that I prayed prayers of protection for him every night while he was away because Mom said war was a very dangerous thing. I had seen an angel in the flesh, but I couldn't tell him because I really don't know him and he might make fun of me, get angry or worse; ask me where I had seen him. I'd be in trouble if I told him it was at Catholic Mass.

"How come some men were killed and some weren't? How come you were kept safe?" I continue to press the question.

"Well, it wasn't because some angel followed me around, Dee. There ain't no angels on no battlefield!"

I look at him defiantly while knowing I can't continue this part of the conversation much longer, so I'd just better tell him what I think. At this moment I'm not afraid. Dad is staring at me and grinding his molars together. He's either nervous or angry.

"Maybe you just never saw the angel, Dad. Just because you never saw him, doesn't mean he wasn't there."

Dad continues to stare at me, but says nothing. I stare back. I'm not backing down, apologizing for acting like a know-it-all, or changing my opinion.

Dad finally speaks, "Well, kid, I can see I got my hands full with raisin' a daughter who's a chip off the ol' block. I think that now ya know a lot about where I've been and I know a lot about where ya goin'.

"Let's hope the seas ain't always choppy, Dee."

Dee and Mae In Upstate New York

The Mathematics Lesson

I'm not going to kindergarten and I'm not moving from New York! I'm determined to throw a screaming fit every time Mom and Dad mention these subjects. This is the umpteenth time it's come up today. I cry and cry until my cheeks are wet, my face is red and I look horrible.

Not wanting me to be upset about the move, Mom focuses on kindergarten.

She says in a compassionate tone, "OK, we'll wait until first grade." Then, ending her streak of compassion and moving into downright authoritarianism she adds, "But then ya have gotta' go! A child needs an education. Forget about the fact that ya think ya know everything because I let ya watch movies at Lowe's while I was countin' box office money and Aunt Yola doled out candy at the concession stand."

Lighting a cigarette with her United States Marine Corps lighter that is inscribed "Semper Fi" (Always Faithful), she drags me down the sidewalk to our old Chevy parked at the curb, and continues degrading my self-curriculumed education. When she goes off on one of her tirades, I have the habit of focusing on some question that is triggered by some visual input. "Why would someone have Semper Fi on a lighter? Why be faithful to a spark, flint or a cigarette?"

She continues speaking as the cigarette flops from between her lips, "Ya need ta learn what they can teach ya in school."

What is she talking about? I'm learning Italian, German, and English. I know how to cook a full meal and I'm only five years old. I think Guinea Red is a fine wine! I doubt if I'll learn the art of a sommelier in school. Besides, what kid my age can make a cappuccino or even say the word? I know how to do laundry, curtsey to the nuns and hold a polite conversation.

Several examples come to mind that happened in New York and I play them in my mind like a newsreel.

Once while visiting Mr. Katz, the furrier, I asked while batting my eyelashes, "How did you make the eyes on those minks look like they are alive, and why do women wear them around their necks like the minks are chasing each other?"

To Mrs. Palmeri, the baker, I asked, "Excuse me, Mrs. Palmeri. What is the plural of canoli and where did the term Baker's Dozen come from?"

Even Doc, the pharmacist, who doubled as the soda jerk behind the ice cream counter commented on how poised I was for a little kid.

"May I have chocolate sprinkles on my ice cream cone, Doc? Um, only if it's not too much trouble."

Even when a most embarrassing topic came up with Doc, I behaved as my Mom would say, like a Smith Graduate, cool and unruffled.

My favorite way to escape trying to figure out what a conversation is about is to go inside my head and replay movies I've seen or listen to music. Occasionally I check in with the adult conversation and whip my attention back inside my own brain. Here's an example:

One day while enjoying ice cream at Doc's drug store Mom whispers, "Doc, I want ta ask ya advice." I look up and see her leaning over the soda counter while she glances around like an agent for J. Edgar Hoover. "Dee and I went ta upstate New York and well, ya know, we're very clean, but it seems she got (lowering her voice) head lice."

I hear "headlights," but I'm too busy eating my ice cream cone to pay closer attention. Acting nonchalant, I use my tongue to make an ice cream sculpture in the shape of the flame on the torch of the Statue of Liberty.

I am wondering: (A) why Mom is talking in a whisper and, (B) what headlights have to do with me.

"What exactly should we do about it?" Mom continues in her stage whisper while lighting a second cigarette as the first one curls smoke from the glass ashtray. She simultaneously checks a bit of chipped nail polish on her index finger and adjusts the alignment of her wedding and engagement rings.

"Well, Mae," says Doc as he leans on the counter like a bookie giving advice about the next horserace, "you have to apply a pine tar product on clean, damp hair and let it set for twenty minutes and that kills the lice. You wash it off with shampoo and, to make sure all of the eggs are killed, repeat the procedure in a week."

I don't know if the ice cream is giving me brain freeze, but I think (somewhere between reality and Ella Fitzgerald's voice in my head) they are talking about headlights and something about a painter with ice. Mom pays for a bottle of stuff. I act like I don't know what they are talking about. (I don't.)

I thank Doc for a delicious and artistic ice cream cone and tell him if he doesn't make it as a pharmacist, he should just take care of the soda fountain because he is a maestro with the ice cream scoop. "Doc, I especially like the way you wrap the napkin around the cone so if any ice cream melts it won't make a mess."

Climbing down from the barstool, I shrug and say, "What more can a girl want in a gentleman?"

Doc looks dumbfounded as we leave waving a fond goodbye; Mom stashing the bottle of poison into her pocketbook. All of these past vignettes flash through my mind as her 'Ya-have-ta'-go-ta'-school' rant continues.

Mom's argument pro-school includes that we will be moving to Camp Lejeune, North Carolina because the Marine Corps is transferring Dad and I will need to make friends at school—friends my own age. I feel this line of reasoning is an insult. I'll be living in government housing with government furnishings and treated like a number in a classroom full of children. Even though I can't read *Dick and Jane*, I can count in three languages, and make up plays in my head. I can tell within sixty seconds of meeting a new person if I might start a meaningful conversation. What more can they want from a kid my age?

Tonight I'm making up the stage directions for "Rapunzel." It's a story about a beautiful, longhaired princess trapped in a tower and rescued by a prince who uses her hair as a rope and, without the help of carabineers, is able to climb to her rescue.

I make the mistake of a lifetime. I admit to my Mom that I intend to hold auditions for cast members.

"How are ya goin' ta find ya actors, 'Dee Mille'?" Mom refers to me, though not in a complimentary tone, as Cecil B. DeMille, the great film director.

"I'll audition them. Just like someone must have done for the Rockettes at Radio City Music Hall, except for the part of the prince. I'll play that role."

"YOU are goin' ta play a man's part? Wadda' ya, crazy? What makes ya think ya can do that?" Mom says as her eyelid droops from the curl of the cigarette smoke pouring into her eye, and ignoring my Rockettes answer.

"Well, I'm the only one with bangs who can put my hair in a pageboy." Mom ignores me again. I had her on that one. Dad looks up from spit-shining his shoes with cordovan wax and gives me a wink as if to say, "That's a good one, Dee."

"Get outta' here!" Ashes are falling from her Lucky Strike like molten lava and I watch what my Dad refers to as "a hot one" fall onto the carpet. I count to myself to see if this spark makes it past six, which is the most time an ash has ever survived. Without looking Mom puts it out with her loafer. "Make ya'self useful and get me a coupla' peanuts, will ya?"

I walk over to the dish and get her a handful and deliver them. "Sauter's Delivery Service."

"What's this? I said a couple."

I look at her, puzzled. "How many is a couple?"

I've heard my parents use this word, couple, but I have never thought about it as a number.

"Two . . . two is a couple. Like a man and a wife . . . two. Like two cannolies on a plate. That's a couple. Are ya hearin' me here? I'm speakin' ya second language."

Shocked, I sit down like a new world has just been discovered and I am on the wrong continent. "If two is a couple, then how many head make one cattle?"

"I'm tellin' ya, Art, what's the God's honest truth. It's time for this kid ta go ta school. I'm puttin' my foot down!"

Dad laughs until he has tears shooting out of his eyes and Mom mumbles something in Italian.

I realize that I have just borrowed one more year without having to begin school, but I haven't figured out how not to move from New York. The worst part is I feel stupid because since I don't know how many head make one cattle, I guess I'm not as smart as I think I am.

Dejected, I know I'll have to begin first grade convinced that I do not know everything.

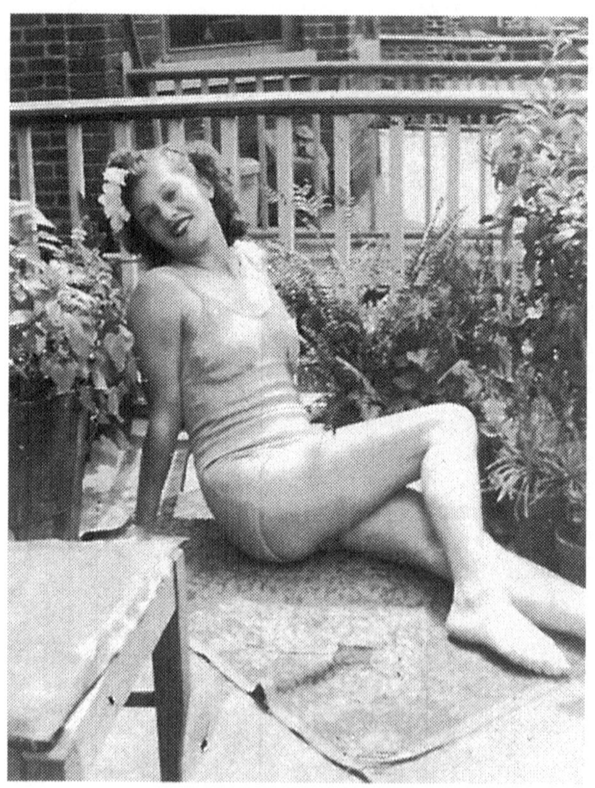

Mae's Pin-Up Photo

Mae, Grandma Catherine (not Steve), Grandpa Albert (Grandpa Steve), Grandma Victoria (Grandma Steve)

The Gypsies

I got in trouble for being a smart mouth.
My Aunt Yola asked me how I liked the idea of moving out of New York and going to live on a Marine Corps base.

As my Mom puts it, "Ya put ya foot in ya mouth! It was the attitude!" she says as she repeats word for word exactly what I said to Aunt Yola.

"What do YOU think? I'll be living on a Marine base in something called a Quonset hut, going to school for the first time, and hearing everybody talk Southern."

Mom does a pretty good job of imitating me.

She continues, "Ya have ta have respect and lose the attitude, kid. Ya goin! That's that!"

I feel like I could cry, but I'm not going to because Mom will say I'm acting.

"Think a' the good part a' the trip," Mom says while tucking my socks inside my shoes and putting them in the suitcase.

"Like what?" I ask.

"Look, kid," Mom says as she folds my sweater, "people move. Families move. Ya father re-enlisted for four years. He's been movin' all over the world every few months. It seems ta me ya actin' like the Queen of Sheba with ya demandin' attitude. We ARE going with him ta Camp Lejeune, North Carolina."

"Can't I be an orphan like some kids?"

"No," says Mom as she stuffs more shoes into the pockets of my brown striped suitcase that is already bulging like a sack of potatoes.

"I've seen it in the movies. Some orphan kid gets adopted and gets to live in a fancy apartment in Manhattan and has a really cute dog," I plead.

"Ya'd miss me and ya father. They wouldn't make ya pasta. They wouldn't make ya coffee and give ya Italian cookies. Ya'd be miserable." Mom says this as if she's making a list.

"Mom, I don't want to be in the Marines!"

"Wadda' ya taukin' about? Ya not a Marine. Ya a kid. Ya a kid who needs ta be with her parents, go ta school and be happy."

"I could live with Grandma and Grandpa Steve in Brooklyn and you could come and visit," I whine.

"Ya losin' it, kid," says Mom.

I feel myself getting really mad and remember what my Aunt Yola always says, "Dogs get mad; people get angry."

I start to sing to myself. It's a song I made up to use whenever I don't want to listen to my Mom. It works. She's lighting a cigarette and talking about how much I'm going to love living on a swamp near Jacksonville, North Carolina. Right about now is when I start humming so I don't have to listen to her.

After I get to the end of my song, I ask, "Is there a mummy in the swamp?"

"Whadda' ya taukin' about? What mummy? What swamp?"

I guess she was talking about something else that I missed when I was humming and singing to myself.

Mom sits down on the chenille bedspread and pats the bed with her hand. "Come here. Sit down. I can see that I gotta tauk ya language—the language a' the cinema."

I sit down beside her.

Mom puts her arm around me and runs her long, red fingernails through my hair to push it out of my eyes.

"What if Humphrey Bogart was movin' ta North Carolina and he wanted Lauren Bacall ta go with him? Don't ya think she'd go? She loves the guy. She wouldn't stay behind and live with her grandparents and she certainly wouldn't want ta be an orphan. Plus, she's only eighteen or nineteen years old. She's just a kid. She can't leave the guy. They're a team. They're a couple. He takes good care a' her. He'd be lost without Lauren."

She looks at me and I see she's wiping a tear from her eye leaving a trail of mascara beneath her lower lid.

I sigh. "I want to be like Lauren Bacall. I'll go. I won't like it, but I'll go. I bet she wouldn't like the swamp either."

Mom ignores me, stands up and starts packing as if we never had this conversation.

"Tomorrow we leave for Lejeune!"

I hear the front door open and Aunt Yola comes into the bedroom.

"Ya nothin' but Hungarian gypsies, Mae. How can ya drag ya kid around the United States and never have a real home? If Dee starts playin' the violin and ya jewelry gets big and fancy, I'll know ya left ya Italian roots and became Hungarian."

"Get outta' here, Yola," says Mom.

Aunt Yola looks in the mirror behind the dresser and checks her lipstick and hair. "Honestly, Mae, ya neva left New York except for the time ya went off ta Hollywood ta be an actress. Ya know that it didn't last very long. I think y'll be back here before ya know it."

"Not this time, Yola. This is different." Mom looks very serious, more serious than I've ever seen her. She continues, "I want ta be with my husband and make a home for us. It's time ta break away from the family and make a new start. Look at it this way. Y'll have the chance ta come and visit and see parts a' the United States that ya neva seen."

I have never heard my Mom and Aunt Yola talk like this. Usually they both talk at the same time and get louder and louder until they are screaming at each other.

I'm just sitting here being quiet and secretly wishing Aunt Yola can change Mom's mind.

"Ya killin' ya Mother, Mae. I can see it on her face. She's goin' ta miss Dee. The house'll be empty," says Aunt Yola as she paces on the rug.

Mom, still looking very serious, says, "I'm goin', Yo', and nobody and nothin' is stoppin' me."

Aunt Yola starts crying. Mom is crying. I know we're going to Camp Lasagna tomorrow, May 20, 1947.

Mae

Mae and Art

Dee On the Front Porch Of the Canale Home

Reveille 0500 Hours

"Reveille in the swamp!"

I can hear my Dad talking to me, but when I open my eyes it's dark. He turns on the lamp and starts to sing and pretends like he's playing a bugle.

"Ya can't get 'em up
Ya can't get 'em up
Ya can't get 'em up in the morning
Ya can't get 'em up
Ya can't get 'em up
Ya can't get 'em up at all
The Corporal's worse than Privates
The Sergeant's worse than Corporals
The Lieutenant's worse than Sergeants
And the Captain's worse of all."

"Time ta hit the deck, kid," says Dad. "We gotta be in my new Ford, pullin' away from the curb by 0600 hours. Today we leave Corona, New York for Camp Lejeune, North Carolina. Duty calls."

Dad smiles a great, big smile and I cover my face with my quilt and blanket, groaning.

Mom comes into my room and brings my clothes—a dress, sweater, some white socks and my oxford shoes made by Buster-Brown-who-lives-in-a-shoe-that's-my-dog-Tige-look-for-him-in-there-too.

"Time ta go. Wash ya face, brush ya teeth, get dressed and we'll meet ya at the table for coffee and an egg," says Mom.

I sit up in bed.

"What time is it? It's dark!"

"Time ta get up and get on the road. Time for an adventure. Time ta say goodbye ta Grandma Catherine, Auntie Olympia and Aunt Yola," Mom says as she leans against the doorjamb putting on her shoes. She leaves as Dad pulls her by her hand. She giggles and they disappear.

I hear voices in the kitchen and smell the coffee. I get dressed and walk down the hall past the vestibule. There are five suitcases and the big seabag Dad had when he came home from the war. I stop in the bathroom, splash water on my face, brush my teeth and wonder what's going to happen to me. Except for Mom and Dad, I'm leaving all of the people I know and might never see them again.

I walk through the living room and into the kitchen and notice all of my things; my books, dolls and toys are gone. Mom has packed everything.

Aunt Yola, dressed in her robe and pajamas says, "Sit down, kid. Take a load off. Ya wan' a hardboiled egg? Nobody's eatin' 'em this morning."

I shake my head, no.

Mom, Dad, Grandma Catherine and Aunt Yola are drinking coffee and eating bread. Auntie Olympia is standing near the sink crying.

Aunt Yola continues, "This is a big day for ya, Dee."

I don't answer. I don't want an egg. I just drink my coffee, eat my bread and take in their conversation.

Dad looks at me and says, "We'll head for Philly and then Baltimore. We'll make a little vacation of it, Dee. It'll be fun."

I don't answer.

Everybody gets quiet and looks at me. I feel very sad, but my Mom and Dad look so happy. I look at the others. They look sad too. Maybe I should stay with the sad ones, but I know I have to go with the happy ones.

Grandma stacks little boxes from the Italian bakery on the table and explains that it's always good to take food in case you're stranded on the road.

The food part sounds good to me, but the stranded part gives me a stomachache.

Aunt Yola tells Mom she hopes the car doesn't break down, but if it does there's always the train.

My head is starting to hurt because I can't figure out how we'd walk with all of our suitcases to catch a train. Mom always empties most of her extra things out of her pocketbook just to take the subway because she says a pocketbook packed like a blevey is too heavy to carry.

I'm getting a big lump in my throat.

Grandma tells everybody to finish breakfast because we have to get on the road.

I'm trying not to cry.

"Ah, we're almost at our expected time a' departure," says Dad as he gets out of his chair. Everybody puts down their coffee and stands up.

They all leave the kitchen talking, but I lag behind looking at the furniture in the kitchen. I run my hand over the edge of the big kitchen table feeling the grain of the wood. I set this table three times a day for the past three years. It was my first job handed down from Auntie Olympia who taught me that silver, linen and china are like precious objects because the food tastes better when you set the table with care.

I walk towards the herb shelves where Grandma Catherine keeps her herbs she calls medicine: chamomile for calming me down if I had a bad day or needed tea to make me sleep, spearmint and peppermint for my belly aches and corn silk for Auntie's swollen ankles. There is a crucifix hanging near the herb shelf because Grandma Catherine says God puts healing plants on the earth and we need to thank Him for these gifts.

I am saying goodbye to all of these things: the pots on the stove, the wooden spoons standing on end in the big pitcher. The icebox drip pan is almost overflowing because everyone has been helping us get ready for the trip. I take in a big breath and smell the room. I want to remember where I lived.

I do the same thing in the living room. I touch the furniture and feel the soft carpet under my shoes. It's worn from where I used to roller-skate. I hear the wooden floors creak. I smell the roses on the round table and touch the family photographs—many of me.

I look at the drapes that I used to hide behind and pretend no one could see me. I love the doilies on the arms of the couch and chairs—the ones I'd put on my head when I'd play dress-up. I look up at the chandelier and see the mistletoe that we forgot to take down months ago.

I stop and stare at the painting of the lady playing the piano and the men and women gathered around her in a parlor. I love that painting. It came from Sicily. I hope I can always remember this room and the days I played in here and the nights we would all gather around the radio listening to music and the news about the war. I wonder if I'll ever see this place again.

I walk down the hall towards the front door and see Dad taking the suitcases out to the car. The rest of us stand in the vestibule and say goodbye. Everybody is talking at once. As soon as they kiss me goodbye, they start to cry.

I'm crying now and saying goodbye and yes, I'll be a good girl, I promise.

We all walk to the curb.

Dad stacks all of the suitcases and his seabag in the trunk and the food goes in the back seat with me. I climb onto my seat. I have my doll and a little, beaded evening bag that Auntie Olympia gave me. She makes these bags for rich ladies who go to the opera. Inside the bag is my favorite thing. It's a little wooden case that I can unscrew and inside is a statue of the Virgin Mary holding the baby Jesus. Grandma gave me this silver, Holy statue and said it would last forever. Whenever I open the case and take out the statue, I'm supposed to kiss the Virgin Mary and thank her for watching over me. I love doing this because it makes me feel good like when I see the angels out of the corner of my eye when I'm not doing anything in particular.

I'm looking out the car door that Dad has left open and see my Mom and Dad saying goodbye one more time. Everybody is crying except Dad.

He says, "We'll send ya a telegram when we get ta Jacksonville, North Carolina before we go on the base. I guess this'll be the first time ya won't have ta worry about getting a telegram in the five years I was overseas."

Everybody sighs and agrees with him.

Dad opens the car door for Mom and then he gets in and starts the car. We pull away from the curb and I look out the back window. Standing on the sidewalk in front of the three-story house with the iron fence and gate are the three of them—Grandma Catherine, Aunt Yola and Auntie Olympia. I see that Grandma Catherine has put up a sign hanging from the front porch over the stoop. It says, "Room For Let." I guess if we ever come back, someone else will be living in my room.

Mom and Dad are right.

It's time to go.

Art In Uniform

Camp Lasagna, Here We Come

This is going to be a long, long car trip. Usually if Mom and I went some place we'd take short trips on the subway. It's nicer in a car because I can sit down and I don't have to worry about getting separated from Mom. She always worried about that.

Today we drove through Trenton, Philadelphia, Baltimore, and finally to Washington, D.C. Mom and Dad talked the whole way. I slept a lot and when I'd wake up they'd tell me what cities we had driven through and which city was next. I didn't know the trip would be so long.

Finally, Dad says, "The hard part a' the trip is behind us, troops. Let's stay overnight in D.C. There are plenty of hotels that'll welcome a Marine Sergeant's family."

I am looking out the window at all of the traffic and the buildings. Things are spread out and there are a lot of trees and grass, not like in Corona. Dad drives around all of the monuments and the Capitol Building. I have never seen anything like it! The monuments are big and the Capitol Building is big and I feel very small. Dad points to a building with five sides.

"That building is called the Pentagon. Someday I'll work there if I pull a tour a' duty in D.C. Here's history right in front a' ya eyes, Dee. These are symbols a' freedom and democracy."

Dad continues, "Ya know, when I was a kid hangin' out on the street corner in Brooklyn with my friend, Dutch, I never really thought about our government. All I ever thought about was puttin' horse manure in Mrs. Kornrumph's mailbox. After we stuffed it full a' manure, we'd knock on her door and run around the corner ta hide and watch her face when she came out on the stoop and smelled the manure. We'd giggle when she started ta yell about the bad boys in the neighborhood."

"I bet you got in big trouble . . . if you ever got caught. Did you ever get caught, Dad? What did Grandma Steve do to punish you?"

"Ah, Jeez. The old lady came over and told Grandma Steve she saw us runnin' away. I was in big trouble. I had ta clean up Mrs. Kornrumph's manure out a' her mailbox and all a' the manure on the street for a week. I guess ya could say that my first job was ta clean up after the horses from the milk lorries."

"I've never thought about you or Mom ever getting into trouble."

"Ah, I was always in trouble. Trouble was my middle name. Me and Dutch used ta pick up cigarette butts under the bleachers in the ballpark, take the butts apart and pack the tobacco in a pipe and smoke it. We started when we was eight years old. I told ya that one before, Dee."

"I don't like smoking. It makes my eyes burn and I can't breathe," I say standing up and leaning on the back of my Dad's seat. "Tell me more about the trouble you got into, Dad."

"Well, I'm just the fair-haired boy."

Dad looks into the rear-view mirror.

"Dee, why wasn't I born rich instead a' so dawgone good lookin'?"

We all laugh.

"Tell me more Dad!"

"Now, ya mother, she was a wild one."

Mom laughs, "Oh, Artie. Don't go tellin' tales about me."

Dad laughs. "Saved by the bell, Mae. We're at the hotel. Let's park and I'll go make sure there's a room for us. On second thought, let's all go in and show 'em what a Marine family headin' ta Camp Lejeune looks like."

I'm really glad we're stopping. I'm sick of riding in the car.

We all get out of the car, hold hands, and walk toward the hotel.

I hear singing. On the sidewalk are three black boys singing and dancing. I have never seen anything like this. People are gathered around them and throwing money into a hat. There is something on the bottom of their shoes that makes a sound every time they take a step.

"Look, Dee. They're tap dancin'," says Mom. "I bet ya'd like ta learn how ta do that."

I feel frozen! I can't move. This is the best thing I've ever seen that wasn't in a movie. Their feet are moving so fast; it makes me dizzy to watch them. There's no music and they're dancing! One of the kids is younger than me, like maybe four years old and he's dancing and spinning around like a top.

We stand watching the boys and I'm hoping this time in my life never ends, but finally Dad says, "Let's go in and get a room and a bath. It's almost time for chow."

"Dad, I want to watch these boys!"

"Not right now. We gotta get our room. Maybe later, Dee."

Mom and Dad pull me by the hand and I strain my neck to watch the boys until we're walking into the hotel and my neck won't turn any further.

We get to the room and I take the first bath in a big, white tub like Grandma Steve has in Brooklyn. It's a tub that stands on little feet. When I come out and it's Mom's turn to get cleaned up, Dad calls me over to the open window. We are three floors up and I look down and there are three boys and a man dancing. They are wearing black clothes and hats, even the little kids. They kick out their legs and throw their arms up and down and out to the side. This is the best! Someone is singing.

"I think it's called the Blues, Dee," says Dad. "I heard one a' the Marines play guitar and sing that kinda' music in a bar one night. I think black folks came up with it."

"Well, I want to learn to do that someday, Dad."

Dad gives me a curious look.

Mom is dressed up and stands with me to watch the dancing and singing. It has started raining and they just keep on dancing! Dad takes a turn in the bathroom and that is good for me because I can keep watching the show on the sidewalk.

Finally, Dad is ready to go. We walk out of the hotel and past the boys dancing and one of them smiles and waves at me. I wave at the boys. I really want to stay here, but I'm very hungry and tired. We get in the car and drive to the restaurant.

On the way there, Dad says, "Mae, ya haven't lived on a Marine Corps base since we were in Portsmouth when Dee was born and then the short stints when I was in First Sergeant's School. Camp Lejeune is a Marine base, not a Naval base. Ya won't see any ships. It's the home a' the Tenth Marines, Second Marine Division. We'll see a' lotta' trucks, Quonset huts, barracks, and Marines drillin' with their rifles."

Dad continues, "It'll sure be different than bein' in Manhattan—no subways. If ya want ta have the car, y'll have ta drive me ta work in the mornin' until I can share a ride with a pung-yo."

"Art, what's a pung-yo?" says Mom.

"It's a word that means a good friend. Like me and you, Mae. Ya my wife and pung-yo."

"I'm sure I'll run across a few guys I met overseas who'll be able ta give me a ride ta work. We'll take turns so ya can have the car a coupla' days a week."

Mom is paying attention to everything Dad is saying. It's a bunch of new stuff for me to understand, but I need to try to remember these things; especially the pung-yo part. I need to make some pung-yos too.

Dad continues, "If we're lucky, we'll get quarters on the base when we get there. It'll be a small apartment or a duplex, but one thing about the military, it'll be clean. There might be a PX ta buy cigarettes, clothin' and whatever household things ya might need. There'll be a commissary for food and probably a gas station. If we don't have these things on base, they'll be just outside the gate in Jacksonville. They call it 'J-ville'."

"One thing ta remember, Mae, when ya drive off the base, ya have ta stop at the gate. The M.P. will wave ya through. It's for security reasons."

"Artie, what does M.P. mean?"

"Military Police. They carry a side arm and a rifle. They're standin' their watch. It's a very important job. I stood watch when I was a young Marine in Annapolis and on the U.S.S. Chaumont. The watch I'll neva forget was the one in China in '39. I was one a' the sentries at the sewage plant. God, it smelled horrible. One day I did an about face and fell in. I was up ta my ears in excrement!"

"Oh, Artie, how awful!"

I have no idea what they're talking about, but Mom looks shocked.

"Luckily, I had my wits about me. I fired off a round and a coupla' guys came ta my rescue. It was horrible, I tell ya, horrible!"

Mom puts her arm on Dad's shoulder and I pat his shoulder too.

"Thanks for the sympathy, troops."

"Let's park here and go eat some chow."

As we are walking from the car to the restaurant Dad says, "After we arrive at Lejeune and get unpacked, Mae, I'll drive ya around the base. Can ya read a compass?"

"I guess I'm about ta learn. If I get lost, can I stop and ask directions?"

"Sure, Mae. We all help each other on the base, but don't ask nobody with scrambled eggs on his shoulders."

"Artie, what are ya taukin' about?"

"I'm goin' ta have ta teach how ta read rank, Mae. No fraternizin' with the officers. I'm still enlisted, but maybe someday I'll make Lieutenant or Captain. Wouldn't that be somethin'? Men were advanced on the battlefield because a' the casualties, especially the officers. I'm glad I didn't make it that way. I've seen enough ta last me a lifetime."

"I thought ya enlisted for just a few more years, Artie. I thought we might find a nice place ta settle down and raise a family," Mom says in a low voice, as she stops on the sidewalk.

She doesn't look very happy.

I don't feel so happy either.

Dad puts his arm around Mom's shoulders.

"I'll tell ya what. I think it's a good job for the likes a' me. I never finished school. After two years at Grover Cleveland High School in Flushing, I dropped out. It was 1936, the year I enlisted in the Marine Corps. I'll never forget it—12 December 1936. I headed for Parris Island, South Carolina for Recruit Training."

We walk into the restaurant and sit down at a table.

Dad looks at Mom. "I don't know what otha' job I could do. Ya know what U.S.M.C. stands for, Mae?"

"Sure, United States Marine Corps," Mom answers.

Dad laughs, "Nope. 'Useless Sons Made Comfortable.' That's what it stands for. I was one a' those sons. The Marine Corps made a man outta' me. I'm proud a' my service ta my country."

Mom lights a cigarette, blows a long cloud of smoke, looks at Dad over the top of her menu, and says, "Looks like I just joined the corps too, Artie."

"Welcome aboard, Mae. What are we gonna do with this little short round?" Dad says looking at me.

"Well, Artie, I guess we better start by feedin' her some meat balls and spaghetti. We're all troops and we're hungry!"

"Mom, did I just join the Marines?"

"In a way I guess I did when I married ya father and now ya part of it, too. There's no more civilian life for us. We're in the Marines now. When ya were born we were in military housing, but I just stayed at home and always thought bein' in the Marines was a temporary thing. Now things are different. I think that now it's our way of life."

I'm feeling like Alice in Wonderland and there's no way out. I was a kid when we left Corona and now I'm a Marine. I'm glad I took my doll into the restaurant because if I had left her in the car, she might be wearing a uniform the next time I see her.

We eat until we have very full bellies. Mom and Dad are talking about Camp Lejeune, money, beds, and buying food for the kitchen.

I'm not too interested in anything they're talking about, so I'll just sit here and think about how I'm supposed to meet some other Marine kids and go to a Marine school. It's too much to worry about. Too much has happened today. I just want to go back to the hotel, sleep until Dad wakes me up and tells me it's 0500 hours, and time to get on the road.

Tomorrow we'll spend our first night in Camp Lasagna and from that day on, I'll probably wake up in the dark when the bugle blows reveille.

Mae's Rude Awakening At Camp Lasagna

The Rude Awakening

I have traveled afar, from the kingdom of Cielo Paradiso to save this fair princess who is sleeping before me. Her beauty is from heaven, her hair like golden ribbons, her long eyelashes outline her eyes that open the way to her soul. With one kiss, I will awaken her. On bended knee, I will fold my arms around her precious body. I will remove her from this tower to which she was banished for not following her parent's wishes. Woe unto them who treated her so harshly when she refused to travel to the far away village. I will place her on my steed and take her home to the king, my father. We will marry and the entire kingdom will welcome my precious bride. She will be my princess and we will live hap. . . .

"Attention, troops! All hands on deck! Wipe the sleep outta' ya eyes! We're here! Camp Lejeune, North Carolina!"

It's my Dad's voice sounding like the voice on the newsreels that play before the movie starts.

I wake from my dream. The prince is gone. I sit up from the back seat of the car and see a man who looks like a policeman standing near a big gate. I look at Mom. She has been asleep too. She fluffs her hair and stares out the car window.

"Are we at the base, Artie?"

"Yes. Look sharp now, Mae."

Dad stops the car at the gate. He hands some papers to the policeman and asks directions. The policeman waves us through.

"Well, troops, this is it. We're at Lejeune—a base built on a swamp. It's beautiful here now, but it'll be muggy in the summer and freezin' cold in the winter."

Dad points out the passenger side window. "In that forest there's deer, rabbits, possums n' skunks. Why, it's a real zoo."

I'm listening to Dad, but still thinking about the policeman with the guns.

"Dad, what do you call that man at the gate?"

"He's an M.P., Dee."

"If we didn't stop, would he shoot us?"

"He'd blow his whistle first, then if we didn't stop, he would fire a warnin' shot."

Mom looks pale and I notice her hand that's holding her cigarette is shaking.

"Oh, Artie, I'm goin' ta have ta be very careful drivin' here!"

"Don't worry, Mae. Y'll be alright. Just don't go gettin' yourself locked up in the brig. Ya'd never make it through hard labor with those red fingernails."

"Arthur!" yells Mom.

"I'm just givin' ya both a hard time."

"Here we are. I'll park here and this'll only take five minutes. Don't leave the car, troops. First Sergeant Sauter'll be right back. I'll go report in."

We wait outside in the car while Dad goes into a one-story building. There are some Marines running down the road. They're dressed in wet, green t-shirts, green pants that have a design like a jungle, boots and dog tags, like Dad has around his neck. They're singing!

"Mom, why are they singing?"

"Y'll have ta ask ya father, Dee. I don't know."

"They must be happy!"

Mom looks like she's thinking about something, but she isn't talking about it.

Dad comes out of the building and gets in the car.

"Well, that's done. Now we'll make another stop and get the key ta our new home and directions on how ta get there."

"Dad, why do the Marines sing?"

"Ya mean when they're runnin' in formation?"

Mom says, "We saw 'em run by the car when ya were inside, Artie."

Dad starts the car and we head for the next stop.

"They sing because it builds morale. It makes each man part a' the team. It builds *esprit de corps*."

"Like the boys did who were dancing on the sidewalk in Washington, D.C., Dad?"

"Yeah, kinda' like that. Only they probably didn't sign on for a four-year enlistment and have their heads shaved."

I don't really understand what Dad said, but I won't ask what he's talking about because we just pulled up in front of a very plain looking, one-story house. It kind of looks like a railroad car.

"Home, sweet home. This is it. It comes with furniture, Mae, so we're set for the night. Did ya bring some sheets n' blankets?"

"We've got what we need for tonight, except for food," says Mom.

"Ah, we'll go ta J-ville for supper tonight and get supplies tomorrow," Dad says as we get out of the car. "O.K., let's go see our new place."

We all get out of the car and walk up to the front door. There is some grass, but no shrubs or flowers. I don't think there is a gardener like our sweet Octavio who helped us in Corona at Grandma Catherine's house.

"Let me carry ya across the threshold, Mae."

Dad unlocks the front door, lifts Mom up, carries her inside and sets her down on the floor. My turn comes next. He carries me inside. I look at Mom. She looks like she's going to cry.

We all stand in the middle of the living room and I know what Mom is thinking. It's nothing like Grandma

Catherine's house. It's just plain and sad looking. The furniture is old and scratched and the sofa looks worn. The walls are gray. The floors look like someone was roller-skating on them for a long, long time.

Dad puts his arm around Mom's shoulders again and says, "I know it's not what ya girls are used ta', but it's our home and we'll make it nice n' comfortable."

I remember what Dad said U.S.M.C. stands for. Since one of Mom's favorite things to say to me is, "Dee, make yourself useful," I don't understand how I ended up here, in the Marines, in this awful house and definitely not comfortable.

The living room is small and in the corner is a funny looking, black, round thing with a big pipe sticking out of the top. We walk into an even tinier room, the kitchen, with a table and four chairs and a black stove and an icebox.

"Artie, what kinda stove is this?" says Mom.

"It's a wood burnin' stove, Mae, just like the potbelly one in the livin' room. Ya have ta chop wood and get a fire goin'."

"I've neva chopped wood in my life, Artie!" says Mom as tears fill her eyes.

"Pull up a chair, troops, and take a load off," Dad says as he pulls out two chairs at the kitchen table and offers us a seat. He spins another chair around and sits backwards straddling the chair and facing us.

"I can see we got a situation here. Where we come from, most of us were born at home. The home was already real nice and comfortable. It's what we grew up with and all we know. Bein' in the Marines is different. Every time we move, we'll walk inta' a place kinda' like this. It'll take awhile, but we'll buy some furniture and have our own things. Right now, ya see, we get these quarters for free—no rent. This is good. In '40 I was earnin' forty-two dollars a month. Now, seven years later, I'm earnin' one hundred and ninety dollars a month. I've done all right by myself and I can take care a' ya girls. So wipe those tears off ya cheeks and put a smile on ya faces. Old A. E. is gonna take care a' everythin'."

I feel sorry for my Mom. She's sitting here in her suit, high heels, makeup and her hair pulled back and two pompadours on top of her head. She looks like a movie star in the wrong movie.

Mom wipes the tears off her cheeks and says," It's got possibilities, Artie. I can make some curtains and get some bedspreads. A few doilies on the furniture will hide the worn areas. Yes, it's got possibilities."

Dad smiles and gives Mom a kiss on her cheek.

"Atta girl, Mae. Ya just earned ya'self a Good Conduct Medal. Well done. Well done."

We walk into the bedroom area and each room has beds and chests of drawers. The bathroom is very small, but looks clean except for big rusty stains in the bathtub and sink.

"Mae, keep lookin' around and I'll bring in the suitcases and supplies. Show Dee her room and check the kitchen. Make sure the icebox looks decent. I'll chop ya some wood so we'll have it for in the mornin' for the stove."

Mom lets out a big sigh.

I do too.

"Well, Dee, ya father is a good man and I know we're doin' the right thing. The most important thing is ta be together as a family, so let's cheer up. I was with ya father in Portsmouth, Virginia when ya were born and we had a short tour a' duty in Camp Pendleton, California when ya father was in school. Those were short tours. This is different because we're goin' ta be here for a long time and I don't know when we can ever go visit in New York. I guess ya could say I'm a little bit homesick, but mostly I want ta be where ya father is, which for now, is here."

"O.K., Mom. I'll cheer up."

Dad brings in all of our stuff. Mom and Dad unpack and I sit on my bed with a book and my doll until they're finished. It doesn't take too long.

We leave for dinner and pass through the same gate. The M.P. is there and Dad stops the car and the M.P. waves at us to leave the base.

"Artie, I think I'll be able ta do this. I'll learn my way around the base before I go ta J-ville. I think we'll all be fine. I just need ya ta drive me around tomorrow so I know where everything is. I guess we'll be here for a few years, right, Artie? When do you have ta start ya new job?"

"I start in three days. I'm Battery First Sergeant. If I'm transferred within the U.S., y'll be able ta go with me. If I have ta go overseas, y'll go home ta New York."

Dad laughs. "Face it, Mae. Either way, ya win."

"Yeah, since ya put it that way, I feel much better, Artie."

After dinner, we go back to our new house. I take my bath and get tucked into my new bed. The sheets smell like lavender water and it reminds me of my bed in New York. It's funny, but I've had another day when I didn't miss my family in New York. The only thing that crossed my mind, once, was that sign above Grandma Catherine's front door—Room For Let. That would be my old room, which is nothing like this room, or this house. Here, it's empty looking, but we have something in this house we didn't have for a long, long time . . . we have my Dad.

Dee

My First Friend

"Did ya wash ya hands and face before ya sat down there, young lady?" says Mom.

The three bowls of pasta and bean soup are sending up smoke signals surrounded by cloth napkins, big silver spoons and small juice glasses of wine—mine is mixed with water.

I look at Mom, hold my hands up and smile. "Yes, Mom, I washed my hand and face."

Dad smiles at me.

"At ease, Marine. As you were. Take a load off."

"I'm so hungry! I've been so busy making a new friend!"

I place my napkin in my lap and fill my silver spoon with soup. Looking at the spoon, one of three we brought from New York, I think, just for moment, about sitting at the big dinner table at Grandma Catherine's. The soup smells the same here, but the house we're in now is very different. We're living on the Marine Corps base called Camp Lejeune.

"Hey, *Che se dice!*" yells Mom.

I have no idea what "*Che se dice*" means, but it always gets my attention.

"I guess I was daydreaming again, huh, Mom?"

"So what is ya new friend's name, Dee?" asks Dad.

"Her name is Poopie."

Mom and Dad lower their soupspoons and stare at me.

Mom says, "That's not polite! Neva say that again! I don't want ta have ta wash ya mouth out with soap!"

Mom has never washed my mouth out with soap, but she's always saying she will if I say bad words in Italian or English, like *goolie*. "Hiney" or "bottom" is all right, but not *goolie*.

"That's her name. Really it is. She told me. I was playing out in the yard and she came walking over to me and wanted to play.

"She said, Hi. My name is . . . ." I stopped.

"I couldn't understand what she said when she said her name, so I asked her to say it slowly.

"She said, "Mm-eye nayem ee-is Poop-ie.

"I said, is that your real name?

She said, "The name I got when I was born was Linda, but my Momma always calls me Poopie."

Mom, reaching for a piece of bread, says, "Do ya self a favor, kid. Call her Linda or people'll think ya makin' fun a' her. They'll think ya got no couth."

"I think she's poor because she's so dirty. Mom, you always say that soap and water are cheap and there's no reason to be dirty, so if she's dirty then she must be poor."

Dad looks up at me and grins as he's taking another bite of his favorite salad which is cold green beans with olive oil and garlic.

"Maybe we could invite Linda to lunch sometime and give her a hot meal. Where does she live?" asks Dad.

"Yonder."

"Is that off base, Artie?" asks Mom.

"It's southern for 'over there', Mae."

Mom looks puzzled.

"What rank is her father, Dee?"

"He's a civ-villain."

Mom rolls her eyes.

"Civilian. It means he's not in the military," Dad says correcting me.

"Oh. So he doesn't go to the wars, Dad?"

"No. He could pick up garbage, work at the base repairin' barracks, paintin'. Who knows?"

I'm thinking of other things I know about Poopie while we all enjoy our food.

"She has one pair of shoes, but she only wears them when she dresses up. She keeps them in a box. She goes barefoot most of the time."

Mom looks at me. She says, "This must be true because ya couldn't make up such a wild story."

"Really, Mom. It's true. Can I bring Poo—I mean, Linda home one day?"

"Sure, if she's outside playin' with ya tomorrow, bring her in for lunch. It's too hot ta be playin' outside between noon and two o'clock anyway. Ya can play in the house afta' lunch."

Mom continues, "Now, finish ya soup and I'll serve the chicken and eggplant in red sauce."

Eating my soup as fast as I can, I ask, "Don't we have to ask her mother if she can come to our house?"

Mom sets plates of chicken and eggplant floating in red sauce in front of Dad and me. She bends down eye level with me and says, "If ya find "yonder," let me know and I'll walk ova' there and ask her mother if she can come ova' for lunch. If ya can't direct me ta yonder, she's still invited."

Dad laughs.

Blowing on a hot piece of eggplant, I say, "This is gonna be good!"

"Ya mean the food or the visit with Linda?" Mom says patting my head.

We all laugh.

Mom is such a wonderful cook, just like Grandma Catherine. I'm kind of daydreaming about all of the good food Grandma Catherine used to make and how good the house smelled when she was making dinner and supper.

"This chicken and eggplant is delicious! Can we have this for lunch tomorrow, Mom?"

"Why do ya want it tomorrow when ya eatin' it today?"

"I was just thinking about how very skinny Linda is, Mom. I don't think she eats much."

Mom puts her knife and fork down and looks me in the eye.

"It's simple physics, kid. When ya eat, ya gotta poo. If Linda wasn't goin' poo, she wouldn't get the unfortunate nickname a' Poopie. So what I figure is, the kid is eatin'."

Mom picks up her fork, takes a bite of eggplant, looks at my Dad who is laughing so hard that tears are rolling down his cheeks and says, "Artie, what's so funny?"

"Mae, ya such a character! I don't know where ya come up with 'em."

I guess this is one of those things my Mom says that I just have to think about before I really understand it. I also have to figure out why it makes Dad laugh.

Dee and Mae

"Poopie"

"Well, I reckon it'd be au' right wit' Momma if I ate lunch at y'all's house. Thank ya kindly fa' askin', Dee."

As we leave my front yard and walk up the stairs to my porch, I ask Poopie, "What kind of food do you like to eat, Poopie?"

"I likes corn, grits, greens and po'k chops, Dee."

I grab Poopie by the elbow.

"Poopie, let's sit down on the porch and talk a little bit."

"I thought we was eatin' just now," says Poopie.

"Yes, we are, but I need to tell you that my Mom is Italian and she cooks Italian food."

Poopie looks shocked.

"What? *Eye-talan?*"

"It's *Italian*. There's a country in Europe called Italy and that's where Italians come from only my Mother was born in New York."

Poopie looks puzzled.

"Uh, huh," says Poopie pulling her mud-packed hair out of her eyes.

"Look," I try to explain, but I can see I'm getting nowhere fast as my Dad always says. "Mom will make some kinda' soup or spaghetti. Poopie, it's good to try new things. One time I tried licorice and my tongue turned black."

"Do ya reckon my tongue'll turn black, Dee?"

I AM getting nowhere fast.

"Poopie, Mom will give us soup with chicken in it and maybe a cup of coffee."

Poopie looks hopeful. "I kin eat soup and drank coffee, Dee."

"Good. Now let's go inside. We have to go right into the bathroom and wash our hands and faces. Then we can go into the kitchen."

I open the front door. Poopie stalls like a donkey. I pull her by the hand into the living room. She stops and wants to look around the room.

"Dee, I ain't neva seen anythang like this before. It's so clean!"

"Keep walking, Poopie. We've got to go wash up. I'll show you my room after lunch."

We go into the bathroom and close the door. I run some water into the sink and put a washrag and some soap into the water.

"Here, Poopie. You wash up first."

Poopie looks at the washrag and looks down at the floor.

"What do I do, Dee?"

"Here, I'll put the soap on the washrag."

When I have it soapy, I hand it to Poopie.

"Here take it and wash your face."

"You go first, Dee. We don't wash like this at my house. Momma washes me in the big tub every Saturday."

I have never heard of a once a week bath, but I don't think I should say anything to Poopie since that must be the way they do it at their house. One thing I do know is that if Poopie comes to Mom's table with dirty hands and face, she'll be sent to the bathroom to clean up, so I'd better take care of this now.

"OK. You know what, Poopie? It feels good to wash my face because it's so hot outside. Watch me do it. Oh, it feels so good!"

I slowly wash my face and hands. When I'm finished, I look in the mirror.

"There. I look five pounds lighter. That's what my Mom always says when I wash off the dirt."

I soap the washrag again and hand it to Poopie.

"I'll bet it'll feel good to you too. Here, take it, Poopie."

Poopie takes the washrag and washes her face, then her hands. The washrag turns brown with dirt. I take it from her and rinse it off in the sink and the water turns brown. I pull the plug and the water drains out like coffee down the drain.

"Now, we can go see my Mom and eat some lunch."

We run down the hall and into the kitchen where Mom is putting soup into some big blue and white bowls. The kitchen smells like chicken soup.

"Mom, this is Linda."

Poopie looks shocked that I use her real name.

Mom turns around to face us. The smile she has at first starts to droop, but at least she doesn't scream even though her mouth is hanging open.

"My, but ya girls look like ya've been playin' in a mud hole!"

"We washed up, Mom. We're ready for lunch. Show Mom your hands, Linda."

We hold up our hands to show we washed. Mom doesn't look very impressed.

"Well, girls, ya made an effort. Have a seat at the table. It's nice ta meet ya, Linda."

Poopie smoothes her muddy hair with her hand.

"Thank ya, Ma'am."

Mom fills our soup bowls and sets two cups of coffee-milk on the table for Poopie and me.

Sitting down opposite us with a cup of coffee and a cigarette she lit on the stove, Mom looks very pretty in her brown house dress, mules, make-up and her beautiful brown hair lifted in front into two pompadours. She blows two smoke rings into the air as she stares at Poopie.

Poopie is eating so fast it looks like she's running a race. Her slurps are loud and long. If my Dad was here, he'd say she was shoveling it in.

Taking a sip of coffee, Mom says, "Tell me, Linda. What does ya daddy do?"

Poopie comes up for air.

"I don't rightly know."

"How old are ya?"

"I'm almost six."

"Well, Linda. Where were ya born?"

"I thank in West Virginia, Ma'am."

"Does your mommy work?"

"I don't rightly know, but she's gone a lot."

Mom takes a long, long drag from her cigarette, lays her left forearm on the table, and puts her right elbow on top of her left hand. She looks serious and as my Dad would say, she looks like she's up to something.

"Do ya live on this block, Linda?"

"Oh, no, Ma'am. I lives yonder by the swamp. Every day my Momma says, "Poopie, I reckon y'all should go play over yonder by them houses, so I come over here. I plays all day with Roger and Connie. Now I knows Dee, too."

Mom seems pretty interested in Poopie.

"What about ya lunch?" asks Mom.

"Oh, it's real good, Ma'am," answers Poopie.

"I mean, who makes ya lunch for ya when ya come over here ta play, Linda?"

"I eat here and there. Momma, she leaves out corn bread and some milk. I ain't neva had this here before," Poopie says as she takes a sip of coffee-milk. "My Momma drinks somethin' like this. I kin tell by the smell."

Mom, never taking her eyes off Poopie, smokes puff after puff. The faster Poopie eats, the faster Mom smokes. She smokes three cigarettes by the time we finish our second bowl of soup and our dessert—a second cup of coffee-milk and two cookies.

For the next five minutes, Poopie talks like the man in the newsreel at a movie; fast, loud and serious.

"I gots no brothers or sisters. I likes ta play in the rain. I likes ta play with Connie, but she shoves me down and calls me dumb. Momma says I should beat her up when I gits bigger n' learn how ta run real fast."

Mom, once every so often, says, "Oh . . . I see . . . No kiddin'? . . . Ya don't say?"

Finally, Poopie finishes her story. It seems she has had three puppies, no birthday parties, no Christmas presents other than an old doll and never had an Easter basket.

Mom gets tears in her eyes and I can tell she feels sorry for poor Poopie.

"Well, Linda, ya have a very interestin' life."

Mom says the word "interesting" when she doesn't want to tell us what she's really thinking about things.

Mom changes the subject.

"Why don't ya girls go 'n play? I'm goin' ta do the dishes 'n bring in the laundry 'n do some ironin'."

"O.K., Mom. Linda and I will be in my room."

We leave the table and walk through the living room. Poopie stops in the middle of the room and her mouth falls open.

"This here is the most beautiful room I ever did see, Dee."

"Thank you, Poopie. My Mom keeps it real clean."

"I'm sho' surprised, 'cause Momma says the dirtiest people on the earth is Spaniards and Eye-talans."

Just when the words, 'dirtiest people on earth is Spaniards and Eye-talans' come out of Poopie's mouth, Mom walks into the living room.

Mom has a cigarette dangling out of her mouth, hands on her hips and she's bending over Poopie like she's ready, as Dad says, to read her the riot act.

"Linda, ya know I got a good idea. How 'bout I run a nice big, warm bath for ya? We'll scrub ya from head ta toe, wash ya hair and I'll wash ya clothes for ya. I'll let ya wear some a' Dee's clothes until ya clothes dry on the line. We'll comb ya hair and put a ribbon in it. Why, y'll look pretty as a picture."

Poopie looks kind of surprised.

"I don't know, Ma'am. I just had a bath last Saturday."

Mom continues the hard sell, "Goodness me, Linda, that was almost a week ago. Let's get ya all cleaned up. No trouble at all."

Poopie looks at me for my opinion.

"Uh, I guess it would be fun for you to wear some of my clothes until yours are dry, Linda."

Mom says, "I'll even iron ya clean clothes for ya. I'm sure they'll dry in no time since it's so hot out there today. Let's go run the bath."

Mom goes in the bathroom and runs the water in the tub. She puts some pine oil in like we always do. The Ivory soap is floating in the tub. Except for some kind of brown stain near the drain, the tub is very clean and white.

When the tub is half full, Poopie pulls off her clothes and throws them on the floor. She's covered with dirt and mud and her feet are so dirty they're almost black.

She jumps into the tub like it's the Atlantic Ocean at Far Rockaway Beach. The water turns light brown. Poopie's got a big smile on her face.

"Oh, this feels real good! It's so warm! My baths at home are always cold."

Mom soaps down a washrag and wipes it on Poopie's hair. A river of brown water falls over her shoulders.

"My God! Linda, ya hair is red!"

"Yes, Ma'am. Just like my Momma's"

I'm sitting on the toilet lid. I never saw such a dirty person in my entire life. I don't say one word because I don't know what to say.

Mom leaves us to wash Poopie's clothes and tells her to make sure she uses a soapy washrag to wash all of her body.

Poopie does a pretty good job. Her feet can't get really clean, but she scrubs and scrubs. When she's ready to get out, I go tell Mom and she brings in two big towels and some of my clothes.

"Well, ya look ten shades lighter, Linda," says Mom.

Poopie, with Mom's help, gets dried off and dressed. She's wearing one of my blouses and a skirt.

Looking at me and smiling, Mom says, "Excuse me, Dee, but I need ta sit Linda on that toilet seat. It's time ta play beauty parlor."

I get up to make room for Poopie.

Mom sits Poopie on the toilet seat so that she faces the wall and Mom can comb her hair just like at the beauty parlor. After she combs the knots out with the big-tooth comb, Mom pulls the front hair back in a pink ribbon and spins Poopie around.

Poopie looks pretty!

"Tell, ya what, Linda. Let's go inta' my bedroom and stand ya up on the make-up vanity so ya can see ya'self in the mirror."

Mom takes us into her and Dad's bedroom and shows Poopie what she looks like.

Poopie looks shocked. She stands there staring into the mirror.

"It don't looks like me!" says Poopie. I looks like a princess! I gotta ax my Momma ta do my hair likes dis. Kin I keeps the ribbon?

"Sure thing, kid," Mom says smiling at Poopie.

Poopie's smiling and I'm surprised at how good she cleaned up.

Poopie and I play all afternoon and have the best time.

Mom irons Poopie's clothes and by four o'clock Poopie has changed into her own clean clothes. Her hair is dry and her face is clean. She looks good.

We say goodbye and talk about playing again tomorrow.

At about five-thirty there's a knock at the door.

Mom, Dad, and I are just sitting down to supper, but Mom gets up to see who is at the door.

Dad and I are shocked to hear a voice yelling at Mom.

"What the fire da y'all think y'all's doin' with my Poopie?"

Dad and I run to the front door.

"Y'all listen here, Wop! Y'all needs ta leave my Poopie be."

Standing on the porch is a woman with long, red hair—the same color as Poopie's. Pacing back and forth, she's screaming at Mom.

"My Poopie's clean. I gives my Poopie a bath every week. It's none a' y'all's business ta clean up my Poopie!"

Poopie's mom raises a fist in the air. Her red hair is curly and flying witch-like in the air as she paces back and forth on the porch.

Dad and I are standing behind Mom who has her hands on her hips and her legs spread a little bit apart, then she starts pacing back and forth keeping time with Mrs. Poopie.

Mom yells, "No! YOU listen ta me! Ya daughter was filthy and hungry. I fed her n' gave her a bath n' washed her clothes. I'm just being a good neighbor even though, I might point out, YOU are from another neighborhood."

Mrs. Poopie moves closer to Mom and screams, "Y'all gots no claim on my Poopie! She's not allowed ta come ta y'all's house no more!"

Mom opens her mouth as she steps right up to Mrs. Poopie's face.

Dad steps forward.

"Mae . . . Mrs. Uh?"

Poopie's mom stops pacing and glares at Dad.

"I'm Mrs. Duquette. My husband works on the base helpin' the likes a' y'all out. We're not poor white trash compared ta y'all."

Mrs. Poopie stops yelling and I notice she's staring into the living room. Mom steps aside.

Dad says, "Mrs. Duquette, would ya like ta come in?"

Mom looks like she could have a few choice words with Dad, but doesn't say anything. She looks angry!

"No. I don't want ta come in. I wuz just seein' how clean y'all's house is. Poopie tol' me, but I wasn't believin' her. Ain't y'alls Eye-talans"?

Mom, a little bit calmer, but not by much says, "I'm Italian. My husband's German. What does it matter ta ya?"

"I declare! I always thought Eye-talans was dirty. I couldn't figger why y'all would wash Poopie and clean up her clothes."

Mrs. Poopie's voice softens, "I ain't neva saw y'alls girl before. She looks clean too," she says looking at me as I'm hiding behind my Dad with just my head peaking out to see the commotion.

Mrs. Poopie's voice changes back into the witch with the red hair.

"Still don't make it right though! Don't go cleanin' up my Poopie!"

Mrs. Poopie stomps off the porch, her red hair flying in the breeze. She's barefoot and talking to herself.

I wonder if Poopie is in trouble and not allowed to come and play anymore.

We go back into the kitchen. Mom and Dad say they need a cigarette and a cuppa Joe.

"Mae, I thought I was goin' ta have ta become a referee or get out my M-1 rifle there for a minute."

"Artie, I was so mad when she called me a Wop! In New York I had all kinds a' friends from all kinds a' backgrounds. We were always polite ta each other. This woman is rude! On top a' that, she taught her daughter that Italians are dirty! Linda said it herself, right here, today in the living room. She had ta learn that from her mother."

"Now, Mae."

Mom turns to me, "Dee, Linda can't come in the house again. I don't want her mom showing up at the door and creating havoc. Linda can't eat here or use the bathroom. I'm puttin' my foot down."

Dad repeats, "Now, Mae."

"But, Mom, it's not Linda's fault."

"Don't tauk back! I'm layin' down the law."

"Now, Mae," says Dad.

Mom looks really angry and when she gets this way, Dad says she's fuming. Mom is yelling and Dad is trying to calm her down.

I may be six years old, but I'm going to tell my Mom what I think, even if I get into trouble.

I yell, "You know what I think, Mom? I think you gave Poopie a bath to prove we know what clean is."

Mom and Dad stop arguing and stare at me.

I'm hot and angry and standing up for Poopie.

"Now, Mae. Ya gotta admit. She's got a point there. Ya won the skirmish, but lost the war. Ya don't need ta be a one-man G. I. party ta get ya point across to the Commanding Officer—in this case, Mrs. Duquette."

I know what 'G. I.' stands for. It means General Inspection. It's the deep cleaning troops do before the General comes to inspect their barracks.

Dad lights a cigarette and then lights one for Mom and hands it across the table.

"Truce, Mae?"

Mom looks less likely to explode. She takes a minute to answer.

"Truce, Artie."

I don't really understand, but somehow this has been worked out. I hope Poopie isn't in trouble. I hope we can play together sometimes. I hope she'll be clean because it made her happy. I hope she'll remember chicken soup and coffee-milk. I hope she'll know this family is clean.

I hope she'll remember me because, clean or dirty, I like Poopie.

Mae's First Holy Communion, circa 1925

The Drags

If I keep my head down, sit here at the kitchen table, drink my coffee-milk, and eat my cookies, maybe she won't notice that I'm watching her. That's my plan. I'm watching Elizabeth Brown.

Elizabeth is the first black person we have ever had in our house. Everybody else calls black people "Negro" or "colored" but Mom and Dad say that's not polite, they call her Elizabeth.

Mom says Elizabeth will come once a week to help clean the house. We will all treat her with respect and be nice. Cleaning is her job and maybe getting me a snack, if I ask nicely.

Elizabeth is the biggest person I've ever seen and I'm fascinated by her skin which is deep brown and shiny, like satin. Her eyes are black, like marbles and her nostrils flare when she talks. She does what Mom calls, 'the heavy cleanin'. Floors are her specialty. Her polishing style gets an A+.

Mom usually does a lot of cleaning, but she has started a new business sewing chevrons on Marine Corps uniforms and she's very busy. All day long men and women come in and drop off or pick up their uniforms. She's got a big stack in the corner of the living room that Dad says looks like Mount Fuji.

I'm more interested in Elizabeth.

Today, she wears a brown housedress, a white apron that she puts on over her head and black shoes that are very run down on the heels. It's the second time she has come to clean. She's real good at cleaning but she does it very differently than Mom.

Mom says she doesn't care how the house is cleaned, just so the job is done.

Elizabeth notices me sitting at the kitchen table.

"Honey Chile, how are yo today?" she says watching me eating my cookies and drinking my coffee-milk.

I look up at Elizabeth and then at the clock. I always have a snack at three o'clock and this is a good time because she'll be in the kitchen with me and I'll be able to watch her.

"Fine, thank you, Ma'am."

"Huh! Yo got manners fo' a young-un," says Elizabeth.

I look up from my cup and nod. "Thank you."

Elizabeth sits down at the kitchen table and takes off her old, black, worn-out shoes and wraps them in a rag which she places on the chair opposite me. The shoes have holes in the bottom and they're all out of shape from her big feet.

"I's gonna wax da flo'," she says ripping up an old bed sheet into large strips.

I sit, staring.

Elizabeth wraps the rags around her foot like someone who has sprained her ankle. When she finishes wrapping the first foot, she wraps the other one. She is humming a song, but I don't recognize it.

She stands up.

"I's gots 'em on real good, chile," says Elizabeth as she walks to the cupboard wearing the strange looking bandages on her feet.

"Now I's needs me some cone-starch."

Elizabeth takes a box of cornstarch out of the cupboard, puts a big handful in her apron pocket, takes another handful, and eats it.

She has my interest!

Humming, she throws a small handful of cornstarch from her pocket onto the black and white linoleum squares. She steps on it and mooshes it on the floor like when my Dad puts out a cigarette on the ground.

I'm still staring.

Elizabeth puts both hands behind her back like Auntie Olympia used to do when she had a backache.

She leans forward, sticks out her hiney and starts to dance.

I can feel my heart pounding. It's like the little black boys in Washington, D.C. dancing on the sidewalk only these steps are really smooth and there are no taps on her shoes. It looks more like skating. The right foot makes a small circle like hands on a clock, then the other foot makes a circle in the opposite direction. She can go forward, backwards or sideways. Elizabeth is very, very talented. I've never seen this even in a movie.

At first the linoleum looks foggy, but the more she dances, the shinier the floor gets. She hums, at first quietly, but the faster and larger the foot circles, the louder she sounds until she's singing.

> *"I'm so tired.*
> *Oh, Lord.*
> *I'm so tired.*
> *Uh, huh, uh, huh.*
> *I say, I'm so tired.*
> *Take me home.*
> *Lord, have mercy.*
> *Take me home."*

Elizabeth is dancing like nobody's looking. She's swaying with her eyes closed. Sweat is starting to pour down her black cheeks and drip down her chest. She looks like she's crying. Down goes another handful of cornstarch. She rests for a moment and takes her apron and wipes the sweat off her face. Then she looks at me as if she forgot I was sitting at the table.

"Chile, I's was in my own world seein' Jesus at them pearly gates. Lordy, Lordy. Amen!"

I just sit and stare at her. The best thing in the world is to get up and sing and dance and she can do it. Oh, I want to be just like Elizabeth! If I had to be black, I'd do it. I don't know if I can eat cornstarch, but I know I can throw it on the floor.

Mom yells from the living room. "I'm goin' ta sit on the porch and smoke a few with Eddie and Jimmy, Elizabeth. Take care a' Dee."

"Yes, um," says Elizabeth, looking at me.

Elizabeth sits down with a thud on the chair next to me. She bends down low, leans forward, rests her giant breasts on the table and looks into my eyes.

"I's kin' tell dat ya got da longin', chile. I's gots mo' rags here. Want dat I should wrap ya foots?"

I pull off my shoes and socks as fast as I can.

"Oh, yes, Ma'am," I say sticking out my foot.

Elizabeth rips some more strips from the old sheet and wraps both of my feet. It feels like I'm wearing tight socks. She wraps over and over again until both of my feet are wrapped. She rips the end of the cloth and ties them in a bow.

"Tries doze on fo' size, chile."

I stand up and she has them just right. This is the best thing I've ever done! My first real, live dancing lesson from a real, live person!

"Uh, huh. Looks real good, chile," Elizabeth says as she stands up next to me.

"Chile, dis' here's I's goin' ta teach ya are called, Da Drags."

"Is it because our feet are in rags, Ma'am"?

"Yo' ain't doin' so good yet, chile," Elizabeth says as she looks at me with sweat dripping off the end of her nose.

"Yo' feets got da rags. Yo soul's got da drags."

I repeat her words, "My feets got da rags. My soul's got da drags."

"At least yo payin' attention which is mo' din I's kin say fo' mos'. Now yo jus watch me. Don't move 'till I's tells ya."

I stare up at Elizabeth. She sure is big and tall. She has tied a rag around her hair, probably to catch the sweat. I look down at her feet.

"First, dancin' is a thang dat comes from yo insides. Enybody kin move dere feets in a circle. Dat don't mean nothin'. Yo gots ta move yo feets wit yo fire dats inside yo heart. Know what I'm sayin', chile?"

"I've never moved my feet with my heart before, Ma'am."

"Huh! I's do declare, chile. Don't day got no heart 'n soul in dat dere New York City?"

"The only time I saw heart and soul dancing was in Washington, D.C., Ma'am. Some little black boys were dancing on the sidewalk. Their shoes clicked."

"Dat ain't no Drags, chile. Drags in here," Elizabeth says pointing to her heart.

"Watch me. Do yo feets like dis."

Elizabeth shows me. She takes her right foot and draws a circle on the floor. Then she takes her left foot and draws a circle in the opposite direction. She looks like she's ice-skating.

"Don't do no neva mind ta do dis' standin' straight up. Yo gots ta bend ova' wit yo hands on yo hips where da fat stacks."

I look up at Elizabeth's big, brown eyes. "What if I don't have fat there? Where do I put my hands?"

Elizabeth gently puts my hands where she wants them to be.

"Right dere. Not too high 'n not too low. Now, ben forwad a little mo'. Yo's gots ta push yo po-po out yonder."

Elizabeth stands up straight and then she shows me how to bend over and stick out my hiney. She puts her hand on her fat stacks.

I do it just like she tells me and it really helps to have her show me, too.

"Yo' looks fine, fine, fine, chile. Now, don't go loosin' dat! Next come da feets. Watch me, den' try it."

You know what? I do it. Slowly at first and then Elizabeth goes faster and I keep up with her, sort of. Oh, this is exciting! I stop and jump up and down!

"Oh, Ma'am. Teach me the singing part!" I say, tugging on Elizabeth's skirt.

"Yo' sho yo kin do two thangs at the once?"

"Teach me!" I demand.

"Lordy, but if Miss Mae come in here, we gots some 'splainin ta do."

"Quick. Teach me, Elizabeth!"

Elizabeth throws some cornstarch on the floor in front of me. She stands in front of the place she had polished and throws down another small handful of cornstarch.

"It's got ta be done over and over 'till it shines, chile."

She bends over and gets ready to dance again. She looks me straight in the eyes.

"Yo' gotta match da feet wit' da song. Yo gotta sang ta Jesus o' it ain't gonna be right."

I whisper, "I'm Catholic. Is that good enough?"

Elizabeth says in a voice that sounds like I committed a crime, "Cath-o-lick? Let's get somethin' straight, chile. If yo ain't got Jesus, yo ain't got nothin'! Try dancin' like a Cath-o-lick! It ain't gonna work! Yo gotta' dance fo' Jesus and nothin' else dat I's knows of! Go 'head! Try it! I's ain't lyin'! Go 'head, Cath-o-lick, lemme see yo soul!"

I have no idea how to stay a Catholic and dance for Jesus, but I'm going to do what Elizabeth says and maybe I'll get the feel for it.

"Hey, Cath-o-lick chile, sang!"

I put my hands back on my hips, bend over, moosh some cornstarch with the bottom of my right foot and make my first circle. I mumble, "I'm so tired."

Elizabeth puts both of her hands on her head and says, "Lord, have mercy, chile! Da Lord ain't gonna listen ta dat. Give it some feelin'. Sang it like yo mean it! Yo gotta' be plum tired!"

I want to get this right. I try again.

"Ma'am, can you do it with me?"

"Chile, dis is what yo call out shinin'. I'm gonna out shine yo'self!" Elizabeth laughs.

I feel frustrated.

"Watch what I's doin' en' jus' do it."

It took me a while, but after many tries, I got the rhythm. Then I matched the words of the song to the way my feet were moving.

Elizabeth stops dancing.

"Praise the Lord!" she yells.

I keep dancing. "Elizabeth, it helps me to count one, two, three in my head while I sing."

"I's don't know about no numbers, chile. Just keep on goin'."

"Jesus, Mary and Joseph!" I say with a big smile on my face. "I'm doing it."

Mom walks into the kitchen.

"Jesus, we got a real floor show goin' on in here! Ya not exactly doin' the jitterbug, but ya look great!" Mom says laughing.

Mom looks at Elizabeth, "I think ya started somethin' here."

I'm so excited that I finally learned a real dance and song from a real person instead of from a movie.

"Oh, Mom! This is so good! It's all right if Elizabeth teaches me to sing and dance, isn't it Mom? It's called the *Drags* and *I'm So Tired*."

"Sure, kid," says Mom.

Mom puts her arms around me and gives me a hug.

"You won't care will you, Mom?"

"No, it's fine that ya learn ta dance and sing somethin' new."

I look up at Elizabeth and she's smiling a big smile. Her white, crooked teeth are chipped, but she looks really happy. She's wiping sweat from the back of her neck with a rag. She sits down and begins to take the rags off her feet.

"But, Mom, I might have to stop being Catholic," I whisper.

"What are ya taukin' about, Dee? Catholics can sing and dance."

Elizabeth looks up at Mom and me.

"Elizabeth, what's Dee taukin' about this time?"

"Well, I's don't rightly know, Miss Mae. I's just happen ta say dat yo gots ta sang n' dance fo' Jesus."

Mom doesn't say a word for about a minute. She walks to the sink and fills the coffee pot with water and coffee. She starts the fire on the stove.

"How 'bout a cup a' coffee, Elizabeth?"

Elizabeth nods, but doesn't speak.

Mom reaches into the cupboard for some cups, plates, and cookies.

"Pull up a chair, ladies. We're gonna have a coffee and a tauk."

Mom brings the cookies, plates and cups to the table while Elizabeth and I look like we've been caught robbing a bank. We say nothing. We do what we're told.

We wait for Mom to say something.

She doesn't say a word. I look at Elizabeth and I can see her heart pounding in her neck. My heart's racing too. I think we're in trouble.

Finally, the coffee is ready. Mom pours us each a cup and adds sugar and milk. She's silent.

She sits down and lights a cigarette. Smoke floats above the table like a rain cloud.

I'm waiting for lightning to strike.

I know I'm in trouble. I wonder if there are any black Catholics. I wonder if the Virgin Mary ever danced. I get a picture in my head of her dancing with a heavy crucifix around her neck and black angels singing. The more my Mom is quiet, the more I start to see things that aren't really there. I look at Elizabeth. She has a heavy crucifix around her neck on a silver chain. I rub my eyes and look again. It's gone. I'm going to Hell and I'll never see Heaven.

Finally, Mom takes one more drag and says, "So, Elizabeth, ya think Catholics can't dance?"

Elizabeth looks sick. She's sweating even more than when she was dancing. She reaches for her coffee cup and her hand is shaking.

"Uh, no, Ma'am. I's means, yes, Ma'am. I means, well, I's don't rightly know."

Mom continues the questioning. She talks slowly, drawing out each word.

"So, Elizabeth, ya think Catholics don't believe in Jesus Christ?"

Elizabeth starts fanning herself with her napkin. The sweat is running down her neck and chest like waves on the beach; one wave after another, faster and faster.

Mom hands Elizabeth another napkin with one hand and takes a drag of her cigarette with the other. Her face shows no sign of what she might say next. With the cigarette dangling out of the corner of her mouth, she unties the white ribbon holding her hair, combs her fingers through her hair and reties the ribbon all the time never taking her eyes off Elizabeth.

Elizabeth finally answers. Her voice is weak and shaky.

"I's don't reckon I's know, Ma'am. I's don't mean no disrespect nohow. I's don't wants ta loose my job or nothin', Ma'am."

Mom slowly puts out her cigarette, drinks her cup of coffee in one long gulp. She gets up and puts a record on the RCA record player.

The music starts. Elizabeth and I are nervous wrecks.

Mom walks over to Elizabeth and puts out her hand. A big smile comes on Mom's face.

"Hear this music? It's called a jitterbug. Come on, Elizabeth. Let's cut a rug! I'll show ya how a Catholic dances!"

Elizabeth looks like somebody just told her they didn't have to shoot her horse. She stands up and takes Mom's hand.

"I do declare, Miss Mae! I's thoughts I's was Bound Fo' Glory any second. My heart's was poundin'. I's was 'bout ready ta run outta' here and neva comes back."

Mom takes her right hand and puts it around Elizabeth's big waist. She puts her left hand out and holds tight onto Elizabeth's other hand. Elizabeth looks shocked, but she's smiling.

Well, I guess this is my lucky day. I not only learned the Drags, but I get to watch Mom and Elizabeth dancing up a storm.

"Elizabeth, you're goin' ta dance the ladies part and I'll dance the man's part. The man's part is called the lead because it shows the lady which way ta move and turn," says Mom as she winks at me.

She twirls Elizabeth around and around. Until Elizabeth looks like she's going to fall over.

"I's feel like I'm bound fa Glory any second, Miss Mae," Elizabeth says with a short breath and a wheeze.

"Don't crap out now, Elizabeth. I want ta teach ya the double turn. Turn up the volume, Dee! We're havin' a party, here!"

They dance, twirl, slam into each other and laugh and laugh. Elizabeth, because of her sweaty hands loses hold of Mom's hand once in a while, which makes us all laugh even harder.

"I's neva sweat so much in my life, Miss Mae. Dis is hard work!"

They are twirling and their skirts are sticking out like umbrellas. Finally, the music stops and they practically fall over, exhausted.

Breathing very hard, Mom says, "Well, Elizabeth. What da ya think? Can a Catholic dance?"

"Lordy, Miss Mae. I's done learnt somethin'. Lawsy, my sweet Lord! Praise Jesus! Praise da Holy Cath-o-lick Church."

Jumping up and down I yell, "And praise The Drags!"

We all laugh and I know that when Elizabeth comes to specialize in floors, I'll get another lesson in how to dance like a black Catholic.

Dee

My Brother, Robert

"I was wondering when I was going to get a baby brother."

Mom and Dad had both taken a big bite of spaghetti. They both stop chewing and look at me.

I'm twirling my spaghetti on my fork.

"What baby brother?" says Mom.

"Everybody I play with has a baby brother or sister. How come I don't?"

Dad puts his fork down and asks, "Why are ya'll of a sudden, thinkin' about this, Dee?"

"I'm with kids every day, but I'm the only kid who lives alone with her Mom and Dad."

"Dad smiles, "What kinda baby do ya want? We could get a screamer, a bellyacher, or a thrower-upper."

"Oh, no. I don't want any of those babies."

"Well, ya never know what kinda' baby y'll get. It's not like ya can send it back," Dad continues.

Mom chimes in. "Mrs. Giordano had twins and it was really hard ta take care of 'em. Imagine doin' laundry every day—all those diapers! Then ya got the teethin', earaches and chasin' two kids day and night. Ya got me spoiled, Dee."

Dad winks at Mom.

"Ya know, Mae. We could adopt one."

"Get outta' here, Artie!"

"No, Mae. How about if we get one that's already about Dee's age?"

Mom looks shocked.

"Oh, I know, I know!" I yell. "Robert!"

Now Mom and Dad both look shocked.

"Who's Robert?" they both ask at the same time.

"He's one of the kids I play with. He knows Connie and Larry. He lives across the street from them. He's very nice. He has good manners. He's clean."

I keep twirling my fork and get small bites of spaghetti and red sauce.

"Well, Mae. Ya know I could go tauk ta Robert's parents afta' supper tonight and see if they want ta get rid a' Robert."

Dad turns to me.

"Does he have any brothers or sisters?"

"Yes, Dad. He has one brother and a baby sister."

"Well, that makes it easy. I'll just tell Robert's parents that we'll take Robert off their hands and take real good care of 'im."

Mom looks serious.

"Oh, Artie. What if they want money from us?"

"Money? They should be payin' us. We'll have ta feed 'im and get 'im clothes."

"I neva thought 'a that. How can we afford another kid?" asks Mom.

"Lucky for us, Mae. Ya got ya sewin' business. We'll save that money ta pay for anythin' Robert needs."

"I was savin' that money ta buy material ta make some new dresses for Dee, Artie."

"Dee won't mind. Will ya, Dee?"

I'm not so sure about not getting new dresses, but I'm real sure about getting a brother, especially an almost seven year old like me. As far as I know, Robert never screams or cries and I've never heard him say that he was sick.

"I think it's better than a baby that we don't know, Dad."

"Well, that settles that. Mae, da ya wanna go visit Robert's parents and wheel 'n deal?"

"Sure, Artie. Let's do the dishes and then walk over there. I think we should just invite Robert ta dinner and not tell his parents about our plan until we see how he behaves himself here."

I am so happy! I've got a really good chance of getting a brother.

Mom and Dad clean the kitchen and wave goodbye to me as they leave the house.

"We'll be back in no time, Dee. Take a load off and read a book, twiddle ya thumbs or play tiddley winks," says Mom.

"Yeah, if ya get bored ya can tear up ya Liberty Card and turn handsprings," says Dad.

Dad always uses this expression that he learned in the Marine Corps.

"Arthur!" Mom says, pulling Dad out the door.

I wait a long time; maybe an hour. I think about how cute Robert is and how much fun we have when we talk about putting on plays on my front porch. I'll have to start on a new play where I'm the princess and he's the prince. I wonder if he would like to learn how to dance and sing. I wonder if he'll miss his real parents. I guess if he does, he can just walk down the street and visit them.

I hear the kitchen door open. I run to meet Mom and Dad.

"Well, what happened, Dad?"

Mom and Dad are smiling, so I know it's good news.

"Robert will be here for supper tomorra'. He likes spaghetti and chocolate milk."

"Yay!" I scream jumping up and down.

"Now calm down," says Mom. "We don't know about him movin' in. We didn't tauk about that."

Dad picks me up.

"Oh, ya gettin' big."

He whirls me around.

"Now go on and get ready for bed. Ya got a big day tomorrow."

That night I'm so happy at the chance of getting a brother that I can hardly sleep, but I do and before I know it, it's time to get up and think about the play I want to put on before I start school in September. I'm so excited.

The next morning Robert is in my front yard. I can see him from my bedroom window. I go outside and stand on the front porch. Smiling, he runs up to me.

"Hi, Dee. Thank you for the invitation to come to your house for supper tonight at five o'clock."

"Robert, you're so polite. Except for Poopie, I've never had a dinner guest who was alive before."

Robert looks puzzled. "Do you know dead people?"

"Uh, not exactly, but I have an angel who comes and goes."

"Oh," says Robert looking like he knows what I'm talking about. "Well, that's nice. I have a pretend friend who I play with sometimes."

Robert and I sure understand each other. This brother-thing is going to be really, really good.

This afternoon while having my snack in the kitchen while Elizabeth is cleaning, I tell her the news.

"A brother? Yo goin' ta buy yo a brother? Yo folks from New York City sho' are different. I's ain't neva heard a' such a thang, chile. What 'bout his kin? Ain't they gonna miss 'im? Ain't he gonna miss dem? How'd yo likes it if yo Momma and Daddy wants ta sell yo'?

Well, let me tell yo', yo won't likes it one bits. Yo be cryin' yo eyes out and so would dey. Da only good dats comes a' it, is dat yo might start ta understan' sufferin'. Yo might understan' the feelin' of the wrench in yo stomach dat won't go 'way. Yo might understan' da low down, dirty blues that comes and never leaves yo'. I's raise' eight chirren and it was hard, Lord, so hard. Most a' da time I's gots no help at home 'cause my Raymond, he was gone, but I's took good care a' mine and never, no, no, never thought 'a givin', sellin' or loanin' any one of 'em out ta enny folks be 'em black or white."

Elizabeth takes off her apron, folds it up and puts it in her sack. She leaves the house without saying goodbye.

I feel awful.

Elizabeth's words hit me hard.

I fall onto the couch. Thoughts fill my head. I think I made a big mistake. Maybe Robert shouldn't come to dinner. Maybe I should never talk to him again. Maybe we should be transferred to another duty station. Why, oh why, did I ever talk about getting a brother, baby or otherwise!

I was selfish. I didn't think of Robert and his family. I was just thinking about myself and all of the fun I would have. I hate myself! How am I going to get out of this?

I hear Mom come in the kitchen door.

"Dee, I'm home. I'm gonna start supper. Ya father and Robert will be here before we know it. Where are ya?"

Quickly, I put a smile on my face. I don't want to disappoint my Mom.

I run into the kitchen.

"I'll set the table, Mom."

"Put the special guest next ta ya place. Will ya?"

"OK, Mom."

Time passes and Dad comes home.

"Hello, troops! How's-a-by-you?"

He kisses Mom hello with a big movie star kiss and then kisses me on the cheek.

"Well, ready for da big meal?"

"Yes, Dad. The table is set."

"Let's all be on our best behavior and remember our manners. Dee, why don't ya go out and sit on the stoop and wait for Robert? I'll go get outta' my uniform and get comfortable."

I wait on the porch step and worry about what I'm going to do if Robert wants to come and live at my house. I don't think it's a good idea at all. I feel like crying, but that's not going to help the situation. Finally, Robert shows up.

"Hello, Dee. It's very nice to be here."

"Let's go inside, Robert. My Mom has made spaghetti and she's warming up the meatballs from yesterday. They always taste better the second day."

We go inside and walk through the living room.

"Your house is so clean, Dee."

"Yes, my Mother is Italian and we're very clean. Every Italian I've ever known in New York's very clean. I don't know why, but they sure are clean. If you ever hear anybody say Italians aren't clean, Robert, tell them it's not true."

"Oh, O.K.," says Robert.

We walk into the kitchen.

Dad says, "There he is. The fair-haired boy. Sit down, son. Take a load off."

Dad pulls a chair out first for me and then for Robert.

"Welcome to our home, Robert," says Mom, serving the bowls of spaghetti and meatballs.

Robert eats like he's starving.

"Put the flaps down, Robert. Don't burn ya self out there. How's ya Mom and Dad doin' today?"

"Fine, sir," Robert answers, keeping his head down and his eyes on his food.

Dad continues, "Robert, are ya sure they don't ration food at ya house? Ya eatin' like there's no tomorrow."

Robert acts like he doesn't hear Dad.

The rest of us eat at a pretty good clip, but take little breaks for a drink now and then. Mom and Dad talk about the weather, the neighborhood dogs, and how busy Mom's sewing business was today.

Robert finishes his food before any of the rest of us.

"Thank you, Mrs. Sauter. That was very delicious."

He gulps his milk in one long swill.

"Thank you, that was very delicious."

"Would ya like more food, Robert?" Mom says reaching for his bowl.

"No, Ma'am, but it was very delicious. Thank you."

Dad turns to Robert.

"How do you like having a brother and sister, Robert?"

"Fine. I like it fine, sir."

I start to feel sick to my stomach.

"Does it ever seem a little crowded at ya house?"

"No, sir. It's just right."

I think I could throw up if I left the table, but I don't want to miss anything.

"Some day, maybe the stork will visit our house and bring a baby brother for Dee," says Mom.

I wish I could shrink down to the size of a pea and roll off my chair under the table.

"That would be nice," says Robert looking at me.

I force a smile.

Mom gets up and clears the plates. I wish the meal was over because I have a sick stomach from nerves.

Mom puts the coffee pot on the stove and places some egg custard in front of each of us.

"Would ya like some more milk, Robert?"

"Uh, yes, Ma'am."

"Ya kinda hesitatin' there," says Mom.

"Well, I like chocolate milk."

"Oh, right! I forgot. I got some chocolate syrup. I'll make ya some."

Mom mixes Hershey's Syrup into Robert's glass of milk, makes the rest of us a coffee and comes back to the table.

Dad changes the record on the record player and returns to the table.

I look at Robert several times and smile. He looks sad.

Mom puts the chocolate milk in front of Robert.

He stares at the glass.

We stare at Robert.

Then I look at the glass. The chocolate is separating from the milk and looks lumpy. I look at Robert. He looks like he might cry.

"Is something wrong, Robert?" I ask, touching his shoulder.

Robert answers in a weak voice—a voice I've never heard him use.

"At my house, we have chocolate milk from the store. It stays chocolate in the glass. It's my favorite thing to drink. I always end my meal with chocolate milk, even at breakfast."

Mom makes a face. I know she could never make it through breakfast without coffee. Chocolate milk would be the last thing on her mind at seven o'clock in the morning.

Robert continues, "My Mother told me to finish all of the food you gave me, Mrs. Sauter, and to thank you and say it was very delicious, but I don't want to drink this milk because it won't be delicious."

Mom and Dad just stare at Robert, then they stare at each other. I know what they're thinking. They always say that they're so happy that I'm not a picky eater.

I turn again to Robert.

"You don't have to drink the milk if you don't want to. Isn't that right, Mom?"

"Sure, kid. Nobody's gonna force ya ta do nothin' here."

"Sir," Robert says looking at my Dad, "what do I tell my Mother when she asks me if I ate everything that you put in front of me?"

"Well, son, ya drank the first glass 'a milk, ate ya spaghetti and meat-a-balls and you'll probably eat that egg custard. That's what I'd say. I'd tell 'em what I ate n' forget about what I didn't eat or drink. If she presses ya for more information, just give her ya name, rank and serial number."

Well, that does it for Robert. He gets happy and laughs with rest of us.

As I watch him sitting next to me laughing, I think about how he needs to go live with his real family. It would never work out for him to be my brother. If he's picky about chocolate milk, he'll be picky about other things like eggplant, wine mixed with water, and anise. I never noticed how sensitive Robert was before tonight. He always seemed so easy going.

Funny thing, you never know about someone unless you invite them to dinner and try to give them what you think they want.

We say our good-byes to Robert. He thanks Mom again for the delicious everything and says he'll see me tomorrow.

The Sauter family pitches in to do the dishes and after dinner we sit around the radio in the living room and listen to a news program. Mom is doing embroidery, Dad is shining his shoes and I'm drawing and thinking about my play that I want put on for the kids in the neighborhood. It's very quiet and peaceful in our house and I think that, for now anyway, we don't need a new brother. I like it the way it is; Mom, Dad, me and Hershey's Syrup on top of vanilla ice cream.

*A Younger Grandma Canale
Holding Poetry Award*

Cheap Travel

I did it again.

Every morning I wake up and I'm in the same position as when I tucked myself into bed. There's only one explanation. I only sleep a few minutes and then it's morning. I've always done this as far back as I can remember. The first time I must have been three years old and I was living in New York. Whatever makes me do it, it has followed me to Camp Lejeune, North Carolina. I'm almost seven years old now, that means that for four years I haven't slept.

This is as good a time as any to figure this out. I'm just lying here in bed in the dark and Mom and Dad are still asleep.

I try closing my eyes for a few seconds.

Now, I open them, hoping for daylight.

No. It's still dark.

I try again. I squeeze my eyes shut and count to ten. I open my eyes and I'm still in my dark bedroom lying here straight as a stick. I haven't moved. I could move, but I'm awake so it doesn't count.

I want to know why I don't move in my sleep. Does time move faster when I sleep? Do I really only sleep a few minutes or many hours?

I'm really confused about all of this ever since Grandma Catherine told me about cheap travel. I think she's the only one who knows about it other than me. She probably only told me because I kept asking her about the clock, if the hands moved faster at night and if it was true that I only slept for a few minutes. In broken English, this is how she explained it and I'm still trying to figure it out.

"When ju-a' take-a da train into da city, ju start-a here an-a da train eet-a' take-a ju 'dare. Da treep-a takes half-a hour."

She sticks out her hand and wiggles it right and left which means, 'more or less'.

I look confused.

"Aspetta. Ju-a go to-a Mass. Ju walk-a wit Auntie Olympia to say ju' prayers. Eet-a takes ju' *dieci minuti.*"

I nod my head yes. "Yes, Grandma. Ten minutes, except for when the angel followed me home and I had to keep stopping and turning around to look at him."

"Dats-a what I try to 'splain-a ju. Angels donna' keep-a da time. Jesus Christ donna' keep-a da time. Only humans ee' maybe some-a plants, herbs, birds and whales keep-a some-a time.

"What I try to 'esplain ees-a dis. Ju go by-a train or walk on-a feets, ju got-a half a hour or-a ten-a minuto by da clock, but no eef-a ju' go by-a 'da cheap travel."

"I don't get it."

"Ju' donna undastan' because-a ju' no pay *attenzione*."

"I am paying attention, Grandma."

I'm trying to think of something else to say as I roll the fabric of my skirt around my fingers.

"So, Grandma, does that mean that Jesus and the angels don't know what time it is?"

Grandma puts her right hand up to her forehead and shakes her head like she's saying no.

"I'm-a tell-a ju' dis to 'splain wha' happens when-a ju' sleep. Ju' travel from-a da bed to-a many odder-a places and come-a back to da bed-a before-a ju' wake up. Eet-a hass to do-a wit religion, science, and philosophy. Too-a much for-a leetle mind. All-a ju' need to know right-a now ees' dat ju' fall asleep, ju' body eeta' stay in 'da bed. Part of-a you brain, eeta' travels."

I can't really understand what she's talking about. Science? Philosophy?

"Ju are-a eein da bed for five *minuti* or-a nine hours. Why would-a ju' move ju' body? You no in it."

"I'm not *in* it?"

Grandma has been sitting in her chair in the living room of her home telling me this story. She stands up and walks to the bookshelf and removes a very small book with a black, leather cover. She walks back and sits in her velvet chair. I'm sitting on the floor at her feet.

She shows me the book.

"*Heaven and Earth,*" she says reading the cover.

"Ju' can no read-a now, but ju' take-a 'dis."

She hands me the tiny, black leather book with gold letters on the front. She has tears in her eyes, so I know the book must be special.

"*Uno momento,*" she says reaching out for the book.

I hand it back. She kisses the cover and hands it back to me staring into my eyes.

"Thank you, Grandma. I'll take good care of it."

I kiss the cover of the book and hold it tightly with both hands.

Grandma Catherine reaches into her dress pocket. She's wearing my favorite dress; the black silk one with the white flowers and lace on the collar and the pearl buttons down the front.

In her hand is a small, wooden container. She unscrews the top. Inside is a statue of the Virgin Mary with baby Jesus. Grandma Catherine holds the statue in her hand. She gently kisses it and hands it to me. I do the same thing and hand it back to her. She carefully puts the statue back into the case and screws on the cap.

Holding the container in the palm of her hand, she offers it to me.

"I have du-a' favorite tings. Dis is one of-a my favorite tings. da book I give-a to ju' ees de' odder. Keep-a dem' always. Take care a' dem'. Learn 'bout-a 'tings ju' don know 'bout—Religion, Science, Philosophy, la historia de art. Don' depend only on-a school. Find-a ju' own-a way. Make-a up-a you own-a mind."

"I don't know any of these things, Grandma Catherine. What should I do? I'll be leaving New York with Mom and Dad. I won't be seeing you very much. What do I do? How will I learn?"

"Ju' start wit' da lesson ju' learned today. Da lesson of-a da cheap travel. Ju' can-a go to da Heaven and da Earth. Just-a remember when ju' come back and open da eyes, ju' are-a back where ju' started, only a leetle bit wiser."

I remember Grandma Catherine explaining cheap travel, but it wasn't exactly clear how to do it then and I still don't understand it now. Grandma Catherine wasn't the type of person who welcomed questions. It was hard for her to speak English and I think she would stop talking to me if she didn't know the right words to use.

There's no one else I can talk to about this. I guess I'm at the time in my life when I can at least try to travel somewhere; cheap travel that is.

I close my eyes very tightly and don't move a muscle. I see Mom and me getting on the subway. I walk by many people sitting and standing and I notice their faces, clothing, and what they smell like. It is all very clear; more clear that when I see people in real life. The colors are brighter, their wrinkles are deeper, their blue eyes are very, very blue, the red hair is bright red. If they smell good, they smell really, really good, and if they smell dirty, it's an awful smell.

Every time the train stops some people get off and some new people get on the train. They look almost like a cartoon to me. Finally, I see myself and Mom getting off the subway and standing on the platform. We walk up the stairs and there we are in the city. I open my eyes and I'm still in bed and it's still dark. I do this over and over again. It's always the same.

Now I'm exhausted. This is a lot for a kid to figure out. I'll try one more time.

I think about Grandma Catherine and wish I could ask her what the secret to cheap travel is, but I can't talk to her. She said I would skip the part where I was on the train. I'd start here in my bed and as if by magic, I'd end up in the city.

I have an idea.

I whisper.

"Gabriel, I need you. Please, if you aren't too busy with the other angels, can you help me do cheap travel the right way?"

I don't see him, but I get the feeling that he heard me.

All of a sudden I get even more sleepy. I decide I'll try traveling one more time.

I close my eyes. I see myself on the subway platform. Mom is not with me. The train door opens. I step in and the door closes. Just like that, I'm getting off the train and standing on the platform in the city. I've done it! I don't remember anybody on the train or the train moving. Just like that, I'm walking up the stairs and I'M IN THE CITY! I see and hear and smell the city. People are walking past me, but they act like I'm not there.

What happened to the train ride? I started from one place and traveled to the other place without being on the train! I want to try this again. For an instant I see myself lying in my bed. Whoosh! I'm back in my bed in the same position as when I left. It's still dark and the house is quiet.

I'm going to try cheap travel again. I go through the same routine, but this time I skip the train part. I leave from my bed. There she is. The Statue of Liberty just like I remembered her when Mom took me there on a trip. At first she's far, far away, but in an instant I'm there looking into her face. I feel like I'm flying. I'm not scared at all. I'm traveling and no one can see me except maybe Gabriel the angel. I feel like Wendy in Peter Pan.

Night after night I try cheap travel. I can go anywhere; even Italy. It's beautiful, just like my Auntie Olympia and Grandma Catherine described it to me. And I can fly over the ocean or way up in the clouds. I never see anyone else flying near me. Sometimes I see cities being built and birds flying in big groups.

I make many trips to Washington, D.C. to see the buildings Dad showed me when we drove from New York to North Carolina. I can see the Capitol and the Pentagon building. Sometimes the black boys are singing and dancing on the sidewalks just like they did when I saw them outside the hotel.

After I come back home from cheap travel, I always feel very little. There is such a big world out there and I don't know where I'll end up or where I'll fit in. Cheap travel is my biggest secret, but I really want to ask my Mom if she knows about it.

One day, when Mom and I are alone having a coffee-milk I ask the leading question.

"Mom, when you sleep, do you ever go places?"

Mom stares at me.

"I stay in bed like I'm supposed ta', kid. Wadda' ya taukin' about?"

"I mean do you ever see New York or the Statue of Liberty?"

"Only if I've had more than one Manhattan; that's a cocktail," says Mom.

"I don't get it."

"I hope ya neva do, kid."

"How long do I sleep?" I ask.

"Ya sleep about eight hours, give or take."

"Do you ever come into my room and see me asleep?"

"Well, kid, I look in ya room when I turn out all the lights in the house before I go ta bed and ya sound asleep in dreamland."

"How do you know I'm in dreamland?"

"'Cause ya always got a big smile on ya face like ya havin' the time a' ya life."

I jump up and run to Mom and give her a big hug.

"Gee, thanks, Mom. I feel much better now."

Mom looks puzzled.

"I swear, kid, sometimes I can't even begin ta figure out what ya taukin' about. I don't know where ya come up with ya crazy ideas."

"I don't think I have crazy ideas, Mom."

Mom lights a cigarette and blows smoke out of her nose.

"Kid, go ahead and give me ya craziest idea and get it over with. I can handle it."

I think for a moment.

"I think I can fly when I sleep and I can go places far, far away."

Mom looks shocked for a moment, but then she bursts out laughing.

"Well, if ya believe those things, ya must believe that a giant egg named Humpty Dumpty fell off a wall and an ol' woman had kids livin' in a shoe."

I laugh.

"Yeah, something like that, Mom, and that a beautiful princess lived in a castle and hung her long, blond hair out the window so the prince could climb up to her window."

We laugh and laugh and hug each other.

"Ya a real character, Dee."

"So are you, Mom."

I think for a moment.

"Mom, did you ever dream about a real woman who lived in a shoe with a lot of kids? I mean, did she look like a real person who smelled like soap and you could hear her skirt swish when she walked."

"No, kid. I never have and I doubt that I ever will. Now, go play, dream, design costumes, build a bridge or do whatever kids like you do. I'm goin' ta iron and get dinner ready. I'll see ya later when ya come back ta earth."

We both laugh and hug each other. I leave my Mom to do her work and I go into my room to think about the play I'm working on.

If the play is about a prince and a princess, I wish there was some way cheap travel could take me to a far-away kingdom of long ago so I could see their clothes and how they fixed their hair, but I guess that isn't possible. I'll have to make up a pretend place with pretend characters and just do my best, but I wonder how the people like Mr. Grimm who wrote fairy tales got their ideas in the first place.

Dee, Waiting For Prince Charming Phillip

Prince Charming Phillip

I waited until the news was over on the radio before I started the conversation with my own news.

"I'm going to be a man," I suddenly announce to my family.

Dad's eyes fly open as he reaches to turn down the volume on the radio.

"What are ya taukin' about, Dee?" says Dad as Mom runs in from the kitchen carrying bowls of ice cream. Her mouth is open but she doesn't have a comment—yet.

Mom hands us each a bowl of vanilla ice cream with Hershey's chocolate syrup drizzled on top.

"When?" says Mom.

"Well, I think I'll start tomorrow. I'll have to walk different, talk different and keep my hair in a page-boy," I say without hesitation.

Dad lights two cigarettes and hands one to Mom. Holding a cigarette with one hand, she takes a long drag and then eats some ice cream with the other.

In a voice Dad says is nonchalant she asks, "'Zat so? Since when does a man wear his hair in a page-boy?"

"I'm going to put on a play. We don't have enough boys and I'm the only one whose Mom can put hair in a page-boy, so I'll play Prince Charming Phillip."

"Charming!" says Mom. "Phillip?"

"Dee, why don't ya let one a' ya boy friends play the part a' the prince and we'll put a hat on 'im?" asks Dad.

"Because, their voices are too high and I'm the only one who has seen Virginia Mayo dressed up in a prince's outfit."

Dad looks surprised.

"What's she taukin' about, Mae?"

"While ya were away, Artie, Dee went ta see a lotta movies. She saw one with Bob Hope and Virginia Mayo and that's all we heard about day and night until we were ready ta scream. It was a pirate movie."

"With a prince? You girls are confusin' the subject and I'm the subject," says Dad.

"Princes have subjects. They're part of the kingdom," I chime in.

Dad laughs and Mom picks up her favorite thing to do while listening to the radio—embroidery.

"I'll go get my papers and show you how I'm going to make the stage."

"I think you're goin' through a stage of ya own, little girl," says Mom threading her needle. "Wouldn't ya rather learn how ta cross-stitch, Dee?"

I think for a moment.

"No, thanks, Mom. I'm busy with my play."

I go into my bedroom and collect all of the papers I've drawn, bring them into the living room and spread them on the carpet.

"Mom, Dad, I'm going to need your help. A play takes a lot of work. I need help with the stage and costumes. Look, here are the ideas. This show must go on! All the kids are depending on me."

Mom and Dad get down on the floor with me.

"Wow, ya have quite an imagination for a young 'un," says Dad.

"What's this? You wrote this play in pictures?" asks Mom.

"Yes, I love the story of Rapunzel. The prince comes to save the princess and she's in the tower. They only way he can get to the top of the tower is to climb on her long, blonde hair. She throws her hair out of the tower window. It's very long because she has been locked away for a long time by her evil father, the king."

"What'd she do, want ta be a man?" says Mom.

"Mom!" I yell. "I just want to be a man for a couple of weeks. Robert says that the actors really get into who the character is and that makes them special. If they don't, they aren't interesting."

I sit back on my heels and deliver the evidence.

"I have to be just like The Whistler or Sam Spade Private Eye on the radio. They have interesting lives and they solve mysteries. Now, that's what I call fun!"

I continue, excitedly. "I'd love to do a detective play with me as a Sam Spade character. I could get Poopie all dressed up in some of your clothes, Mom, and your high heels. Maybe you could do her hair and put some make-up on her. She could be the pretty woman who needs a Private Eye. Maybe somebody is blackmailing her and. . . ."

"Slow down there, Dee," says Mom.

"We haven't heard about Linda in several weeks. Has her mother quit screamin' about how we done her wrong at the Sauter household?" asks Dad.

"Yes. Poopie says her mother is real sorry about being ugly to you, Mom."

"Artie, what does it mean, being ugly?"

"It's southern for bein' mean and hateful, Mae."

"Well, I'd agree with that!"

"Mae, it's all water unda' the bridge. Folks need ta get along. There are too many battles in this world. We don't want ta be angry at Linda. That kid needs all the help she can get. She's welcome ta be in the play and maybe her mother will come ta see the big doins' on openin' night."

"Dad, can you help me tie a clothes line to the front porch across the top step so we can have a curtain in front of the stage?"

"Sure. Mae, do we have a sheet we can use? Can ya make a hem in the top a' the sheet so we can string it up?"

"Puffing away on her cigarette Mom says, "We can use those big safety pins that I use ta pin the chevrons ta the sleeves a' the uniforms. We'll put a lot a' pins in the top a' the sheet and string it on the clothes line. That way ya can drag the sheet open and closed."

"Mae, ya not only beautiful and funny, but now ya a stage designer."

"Mom, how about the costumes? Can you make a princesses' dress and some kind of blouse for me and tight pants? I need them really tight. Is there any way to make me a hat with a feather?"

"Ya know, I got a hat with a big feather. Ya can use that. I can make anything ya want, kid. I'm pretty caught up sewin' chevrons on uniforms right now."

We're all getting excited!

Mom brings out some fabric and drapes it around my chest and shoulders. Dad takes off his belt and puts it around my waist while Mom goes into her closet and gets the hat. I put on a pair of Dad's civilian shoes.

"Ya know, I got a coupla' belt buckles that I can tie ta those shoes. We'll put ya in a coupla' pair a' heavy socks ta fill up the space too."

I get into this temporary costume and go into Mom and Dad's bedroom and look in the vanity make-up mirror. Mom folds my hair underneath to form a pageboy hairdo and holds it in place with some bobby pins. Looking back at me from the mirror is a handsome prince.

"Ya as handsome as the day is long, Dee," says Dad.

"A real lover boy!" says Mom.

I lower my voice, "My subjects!" I yell.

We all laugh as hard as we can. This is fun!

I throw my arms around my Mom and Dad and say, "I'm the luckiest girl in the world! Thank you! Thank you for letting me be a boy!"

As Mom and Dad walk out of the bedroom holding hands, I'm admiring myself in the vanity mirror. I don't really understand what Dad means when he says, "At least she doesn't need a jock strap, Mae."

Mom yells, "Oh, Arthur! Stop that!"

I hear them laughing in the hall, but I'm too busy practicing bows to try to figure out what they're talking about. I'm too busy being a prince.

The Stage In Winter

Finale

I've got a problem. I don't have a king.

I mean I don't have anybody who can play the part of the king in my play.

I need a really big person, a grown-up, not just one of the kids. You see, the king rules the kingdom and has put his daughter in the tower. He's supposed to have a big, booming voice. He's mean. He's tough. He holds a ruler over all of his subjects.

I've got one week until the play begins. I'm getting nervous. I've got to get a king!

I'm pacing around in my room. I've got drawings of costumes all over my floor. I've got pictures of each scene. I can't write a script because I can't write very well because I haven't started first grade yet, but it doesn't matter because the kids in the play can't read.

My plan is to tell them what to say and have them memorize the words. I've tested them all. Here's how.

One at a time I talked to them.

"This is a test. If you can say all of these words, you can be in the play. If you can't, you're in the audience. Now, say apple, banana, cookie and pasta fassolli."

Most of them messed up on the last one, but they got a part anyway.

Right now, I'm in my room, pacing and praying.

"Mary, Queen of Heaven, send me a king. I'm so exhausted! I need help. Please answer my prayer or ask Jesus to send me a king, if he's not too busy. Jesus, I mean."

I've got to get some milk and cookies and think. Think!

I walk to the kitchen talking to myself.

"I need a king! I NEED a king!"

I stop in my tracks when I see the one person who might be the answer to my prayer. It's Elizabeth, wonderful, wonderful, Elizabeth. Maybe I can convince her to. . . .

"Hi, chile. How yo dis time?"

I'm looking at hope!

"Fine, Ma'am. How are you?"

"I's fine, jus' fine as kin be. What yo doin'? How yo doin'?"

I look at her like a cat stalking a bird.

"Not so good," I say with a weak, sad voice. I try to get tears in my eyes. They get a little watery.

Elizabeth looks concerned.

"You see, Miss Elizabeth, I have a problem."

I try to look more sad and pathetic.

"Chile, yo is too much a young un' ta have a problem. What's in yo head? Yo looks like yo lost yo best frien'."

"Well, I'm putting on this play in one week just before first grade starts. It's going to be on our front porch. It's about a princess who's locked in a tower and a handsome prince comes to save her because her father, the king, wants her to marry a very old prince."

"Dat's whatcha call a dee-lemma," says Elizabeth as she sits down at the kitchen table opposite me.

"Oh, it's worse than that. If I don't find somebody to be the king, I can't put on the play. Mom is helping with the costumes and Dad is helping get the curtain and the stage ready."

"What 'bout yo friend, Larry with da red hair?"

"Larry has freckles and red hair. He looks very young *and* has a squeaky voice. Larry can't be the king, Elizabeth."

"Huh! How 'bout dat nice young man, Robert. Yo knows, da one yo wanted fo' yo brotha?"

I level a look at Elizabeth like I know everything and she knows much less. If Mom saw me doing this, I'd be in big, big trouble.

"If I had to yell at Robert, he'd start crying. Kings shouldn't be crybabies. If it was too hot on the porch, he'd leave. If he didn't get the right chocolate milk, he'd throw off his crown and walk off the stage. Robert is not the answer and I'm glad he didn't become my brother."

I walk over to Elizabeth and put my hand on her big, round shoulder. I look her directly in the eyes. I give her the hard sell.

"Elizabeth, if you could help me just this once and be in the play and be the king, I promise to help you do the cleaning for a month."

Elizabeth looks surprised.

"Lawzie! Me? In a play? A king? A white chile? Helpin' clean?"

Elizabeth rambles on and on.

"Lordy, I done' know nothin' 'bout no plays, chile. No, no, I neva got no chance ta read . . . ."

I interrupt.

"Oh, you don't have to read anything because I can't read either. I'll tell you what to say and then we'll practice together, while you're cleaning."

"What kinda thangs will I have ta say?"

I walk behind her and around to her other shoulder and give her a serious look. She doesn't move her head, but her eyes must follow me because she's staring at me when I get to her other side.

"Do you mean that you'll do it?"

Elizabeth has a look on her face like she's holding the best card in the deck like when Mom, Dad and I play Canasta and one of them is about to win the hand.

"I ain't sayin' yes, but I ain't sayin' no, chile," says Elizabeth as she tucks some loose hair under the rag on her head.

"Gimme a samplin'."

She's got me for now. I have to make this sound good.

"Well, Elizabeth, you'd say things like this."

I clear my throat and lower my voice.

"I am the King of Corona and I rule all of the subjects in the land."

I start pacing around the kitchen and drape a kitchen towel around my shoulders trying to make some kind of costume.

I continue, "My daughter is the fairest in all the land. She is beautiful and wise, but she wants to marry a regular man instead of the prince I picked out for her. Woe be to her."

Elizabeth's eyes are as big as saucers.

I pace back and forth some more and point to the ceiling in the kitchen.

"I put her in yon tower in the room at the top. She cannot get out. I bring her food and water every day and ask her to change her mind."

I turn around quickly, flick my towel like it's a cape and whisper to Elizabeth.

"Pretend you're the Princess, Elizabeth, but you don't have to say anything."

I continue, lowering my voice again. I get so close to Elizabeth, if she was wearing glasses, they'd fog up just like Auntie Olympia's used to do.

"My child, please marry Prince Ferdinand. I know he's very old and he has bad teeth, but he is very rich and can put you on a throne and give you jewels."

Elizabeth blinks several times. She begins to speak, but I put my hand up to her mouth to keep her quiet.

"If you do as I tell you, Princess Connie, I will give you a big wedding and buy you the finest dress and carriage and horses. All of your friends can come and bring you a lot of presents and money, just like at an Italian wedding. You will get many bags full of gold and silver."

I back away from Elizabeth, sit down, take a big gulp of milk, and stare long and hard into her eyes.

"Well, what do you think, Elizabeth? Can you do it? Can you be the king? Can you sit on a chair on the porch with a cape and a crown?"

I pause, lean forward and say, "Can you be a . . . *star*?"

"Lord have mercy, chile! I ain't neva bin axed questions likes dose befo'!"

"Say yes, Elizabeth. You can do it!"

Elizabeth hesitates.

"Maybe you could stay here after you, uh we, finish cleaning the house and I could help you learn the words."

Elizabeth still doesn't speak.

"Oh, are you not sure because you have to get home to cook dinner for your husband?"

Elizabeth looks sad, hesitates, but finally speaks.

"Lawsey, no, chile. My Raymond, he on da road."

"Oh, I forgot. I remember when Grandma Sauter visited us and asked you about your husband. She said he was a traveling salesman. I guess he isn't home very much."

Elizabeth looks sad.

"No, chile. He hadn't been home fa' six years. He on da chain gang in prison, yo knows . . . on da road."

I think a chain gang is a bad thing for Mr. Raymond. I guess that's why Elizabeth works so hard to make money. I feel sorry for her, too.

"Oh, Elizabeth! When will Mr. Raymond be home?"

"Chile, I don' rightly know. It's a sad, sad, thang."

I want to know what Mr. Raymond did to have to go to prison, but I know it's not polite to ask personal things about somebody.

Elizabeth and I sit at the kitchen table. We're quiet and just thinking. She gets tears in her eyes and has to blow her nose.

Finally Elizabeth speaks.

"Yo' knows. Might be a good time ta play pretend, yes chile, a good time ta have me some fun. I believe I kin do it, chile."

I'm so happy! I throw my arms around Elizabeth's big arm and hug her.

"Oh, thank you, Elizabeth. Thank you so much. I needed a king so bad. You've saved the play! You're a hero!"

Elizabeth pats me on the head.

"Yo's gots ta hep me, chile. Yo's gots ta hep me rememba da words."

"I will. We'll practice and even if they aren't the exact words, Elizabeth you can say whatever sounds kind of like what I'm saying. Remember, I really need a low, man's voice; just like a king would have."

Elizabeth lowers her voice.

"Da' Kang'll do her best!"

We both laugh.

"Elizabeth, can we start after work today?"

"Sho' nuf'," answers Elizabeth.

I run into Mom's room where she's sewing on the Singer sewing machine. She's working on the princess's dress.

"Mom, Elizabeth is going to be the king!" I say jumping up and down. "Can you make her a cape and crown?"

Mom is sewing with a cigarette dangling out of the corner of her mouth. Ashes are falling on the fabric, but none cause a fire. She needs both hands to feed the fabric through the foot and needle of the machine. I don't know why she doesn't use the ashtray nearby.

"I better measure her head," Mom says as the cigarette flaps up and down.

I notice Mom has one eye closed because the smoke is aiming right for it. She stops sewing, removes the cigarette and puts it out. She looks up at me.

"Wait a minute, kid. Elizabeth? The king? Ya got a problem, kid."

"What do you mean, Mom?"

"Well, in case you haven't noticed, Elizabeth is black and the princess is, Connie, right?"

I nod yes.

Mom hesitates a minute before she says, "Connie is white."

"So?" I ask.

Mom levels a look at me, "So?"

"I don't get it, Mom."

"Yeah, kid. I can tell ya don't get it. The princess is the kings' daughter. They are related."

I have a blank look on my face. I don't know what to say.

"Look, kid, it's like if I was black and you were white. Get it?"

"Well, Mom, you're Italian and Dad is German so that makes me half Italian and half German."

"Kid, we look like each other!"

"Yeah, but you told me I was different from the rest of the family when you told me I was born with a silver spoon in my mouth, but it wasn't your spoon."

"Whadda ya taukin' 'bout this time? What does a spoon have ta do with a black person?"

"I don't know, Mom."

"I feel like I'm in an Abbott and Costello movie! Who's on first? No, what's on first. Who's on second," says Mom.

"I don't get it, Mom."

"I know, kid. I know. Look, you'll just have ta keep Elizabeth as the king, but be prepared ta answer questions from the audience."

"What kind of questions," Mom?

"Look, let's tauk about the crown and forget the lesson about the family tree."

I'm parading around the room with fabric around my shoulders and practicing bows.

"We don't have any trees in the play, Mom."

"Kid, get outta' here and go get Elizabeth before I crown ya!"

I get the feeling not to ask what 'crowning me' means. I go get Elizabeth.

Elizabeth is finishing folding rags and getting her shoes out of a pillowcase. She's off work now.

"Elizabeth, Mom wants you to go into her room and have your head measured."

Elizabeth gives me a curious look and we go into Mom's room.

Mom looks up as she blows cigarette smoke out of both nostrils.

"All hail the king!"

We laugh. Elizabeth's head gets measured. Mom writes the number on a piece of paper and throws some fabric around Elizabeth's shoulders.

"Ya make a fine king, Elizabeth."

Elizabeth laughs. "If only my Raymond was here ta see dis'."

Days go by and I work with each actor.

Today is the first day I have them all on stage and tomorrow is opening night, after supper.

Connie is her usual, mean self and wants to be bossy and change everything. Her princess's hat is too small. Mom blames it on her naturally curly hair. It's too thick and the hat keeps falling off her head. Personally, I think it's the mop head on top of her hair that's the problem, but nobody wants to talk about that. Mom tied long strips of rope to the mop to make what's supposed to be hair that touches the floor when Princess Connie stands on the third step of the ladder.

"Hey, smartie pants," says Connie glaring at me. "I'm not kissing the prince and I know you're playing the part of the prince, Dee."

"Well, I don't want to kiss you either, so we'll just have to kiss the air like ladies do when they don't want to get lipstick on each other," I say rather than punching her which is what I feel like doing.

Connie throws another horrible look at me.

"I don't want to be on this stupid ladder either."

"Connie, you're supposed to be in a tower up high, so shut up or I'll have Poopie be the princess."

Connie turns beet red in the face and makes a fist.

I walk away. I've seen her fight before and give a kid a bloody nose.

This is the way my afternoon goes:

Larry refused to be a horse. How can the prince come to rescue the princess without a horse? I'll have to convince Larry.

Poopie says playing the part of a person in the village isn't good enough and her mom says I'm treating her like poor white trash. I love Poopie. Why would I treat her like white trash, especially since I don't know what white trash is anyway?

Robert is supposed to be the guard in the tower, but his mom won't let him hold a pretend gun. She wants him to be a doctor. I don't have a doctor in the play, so I don't know what I'm supposed to do to stop his mom from giving me a hard time.

This came up yesterday and I talked it over with my Dad. He said Robert should be a headshrinker. That's what my Dad calls a psychiatrist. That way he could shrink his own head and stop being a sissy.

Patty Harden is the new kid on the block. She's very shy. I put her in the part of the queen. She doesn't seem happy to be married to Elizabeth, the King. Patty is very short and won't say anything, but she'll sit on her throne; one of the kitchen chairs draped with fabric. Sitting next to Elizabeth, Patty looks like a doll. She has left her chair two times to go to the bathroom. I know that Mom followed her into the house to listen for the water running in the sink after the toilet flushed to make sure Patty washed her hands. Mom is the military police of hand washing. Every time Patty comes back to sit on her throne, she keeps fiddling with her crown until I want to smack her.

Mom sees me getting a temper.

She whispers, "Ya know, Dee, Patty's a good kid, but she's got a case a' nerves in her stomach."

I really don't care.

As Mom always says when she's at the end of her rope, "I'm ready for Bellevue Mental Ward. Send me ta the looney bin and hose me down with a fire hose."

By the time I'm an hour into the rehearsal, I know why Mom smokes and I think I'd smoke if I was a grown-up having to put up with these grumpy actors.

I stand in front of the stage, short-tempered.

I yell, "Listen everybody, we have to start at the beginning of the play and try to get to the end without you telling me you're too hot, too thirsty, that your costume isn't right, or you have to go to the bathroom . . . and QUIT STARING AT THE KING!"

Elizabeth smiles a toothy smile. I think she likes the attention.

I walk over to Larry who is sitting on the ground talking to himself.

"Larry, this is your last chance. Do you want to be the horse, or don't you? I don't have all day."

"Horses are stupid," growls Larry.

"Oh, yeah? Well, if horses are stupid, why do they stand very still on the sidewalk in New York and let kids sit in their saddles and have their pictures taken? Huh, Larry?"

Larry glares at me, throws the white sheet over his back and gets down on all fours.

"O.K. Thanks, Larry."

"I'm the prince and I'll just pretend to sit on your back and you slowly walk over to the porch. First, let me talk to the king and the princess. I'll be back. Don't go away. You can take the sheet off and rest for a minute.

Larry sits down and continues to glare at me.

I get up on stage and walk over to Princess Connie.

She looks like she could spit.

"Look, Connie, you're the star of the show. The beautiful princess is always the star. If the play is going to be good, it's all because of you."

"You look just like a real princess." (I lie.)

"You're beautiful." (Another lie.)

Princess Connie is smiling and fixing her mop hair.

"O.K. I can do it, Dee. Just tell me what to say when it's my turn."

I walk away from Connie, feeling badly that I lied, but I have to put her in a good mood.

Now, to the king.

I walk over to Elizabeth who's sitting on her throne with her cape and crown. The crown is kind of crooked, but I don't want to let on anything is wrong.

I whisper. "Look, Elizabeth, you're the star of the show. The king is always the star. If the play is going to be good, it's all because of you."

"Lawsy, chile, I's needs me some hep."

"I'll help you, Elizabeth. You'll be the best king there ever was."

Elizabeth smiles a big-tooth smile.

I leave Elizabeth and go on to Robert.

Robert is sitting on the step. When it's time to start the play, his job is to pull the sheets, our curtain, to one side on the clothesline that Dad rigged up yesterday.

When the play is over, he'll pull the curtain closed and then when the actors are going to bow to the audience, he'll open it again.

I look Robert into the eyes.

He looks at me like he's going to cry.

"I want to be able to have a part too, Dee. I want to say some words. I don't want to just pull the curtain back and forth."

I put my hand on his shoulder.

"Look, Robert, you're the star of the show because you have two jobs. You pull the curtain and then you run down the stairs and stand next to Poopie and you are a town person. You say, 'hail to the king and queen' when Poopie says it. This is very important. If the play is going to be good, it's because of you."

Robert is now smiling and giving me a hug.

"Oh, thank you, Dee. This is better than delicious!"

I'm not sure what Robert's talking about, so I move back to King Elizabeth.

Everybody is talking and whining except Elizabeth who is fanning herself with a piece of square flypaper.

"Elizabeth, it's time to say your lines. Ready?"

"I's bin practicin'. If-in I's needs me some hep, will yo hep me?"

"Sure, Elizabeth."

I yell, "Quiet everybody. We're going to start."

I'm amazed. Everybody gets quiet. Mom is taking a seat on a blanket in the front yard. She looks happy.

Five other women are sitting with her and lots of small kids are running around throwing dirt clods at each other. One of the women has handed out drinks that look like lemonade and I wish I could stop for a drink and a rest, but the show must go on. I can't believe that people are coming to see the rehearsal. It's not time for the performance yet.

Mom smiles and says, "Oh, everybody looks absolutely wonderful in their costumes. Dee, fix ya belt."

"Mom!" I moan. "I'm busy!"

Mom lights a cigarette and calms down. "I was just tellin' ya so ya sword wouldn't stick out so funny."

I don't have time to mess with my belt and sword right now.

I continue with Elizabeth.

"O.K. Elizabeth. When I point, you say your first line."

Elizabeth nods. "Yo' means, I's da king?" she whispers.

I don't want to get into some big discussion with Elizabeth.

I point.

"Go!"

In the biggest voice I have ever heard come out of Elizabeth, she says,

"I's da King a' Corona. I's rules all da subjects in da lan. My girl, da Princess Connie? Well, she da fair maid 'a da land. She be pretty and smart. She wants ta marry a reglar man, not a prince what I pick fa' her. Woe, woe I say, woe, woe, woe be's ta dat chile!"

With each 'woe', Elizabeth gets louder and louder.

I look at all of the other actors. They are standing around with their mouths hanging open. Princess Connie gives me a threatening look which I take to mean she's going to jump off of the ladder and cause a scene. She'll scream, sprain her ankle, and blame it on me. She hates the play already.

Larry-The-White-Horse, is laughing and rolling around on the ground. I could kill him!

I glance at Mom and she's clapping with a big smile on her face. She knocks her cigarette with her hand and a big ash sets a small fire on the blanket, but she puts it out with her shoe. She gets the little kids' attention with the flame and they sit down.

Elizabeth continues in a loud, booming voice.

"Y'all listen here! I's put da chile in the tower over yonda'. She be at the top and cain't git out. When I's feels likes it, I's brang her greens and chitlins ta makes her change her mind. I 'splain ta her. Chile, don' have no never mind if dat man, da prince I pick fa' yo', he be ol' n' tired."

I frown at Elizabeth and shake my head, no. I did <u>not</u> tell her to say that last part.

She ignores me and keeps going.

"I's say ta her. Please, chile, go on an' take up wit Prince Fer-din-anns. Chile, I knows he bees old and have no teeth, but lawsy, he be *rick* and gots a throne fa' ya and lots a' jewry."

I'm so shocked, I can't get out any words. I have never thought Elizabeth's words would come out this way, even though I know she talks that way naturally. What was I thinking making her the king? I'm a failure.

I look at the kids in the play and if they had been laughing, they've stopped. They look like they are really paying attention to Elizabeth. Maybe this can work after all.

Elizabeth looks very proud of herself.

She continues, "Chile, say yea, jus' say yea, y'all be hitched ta the ol' guy. Yo do dat 'n I put on a big hoedown of a weddin'. I git yo a pretty dress n' crown. Yo will look fine, fine, fine! Yo understand? Yo sujects'll brang yo big sacks o' money like them dar Eye-talans do it in dat dar New York City."

I look at the audience. There's not a sound. As Dad would say, they look like they're catching flies. They are all sitting as still as can be and every one of them have their mouths hanging open. They look like they have never heard a story told like this.

I'm feeling the same way, but Elizabeth has their attention. She reminds me of the Nuns in Catechism class only she doesn't have to smack a ruler on the desk to get everybody's attention to be quiet.

It's on with the show.

I straddle Larry-The-White-Horse and yell, "To the tower to save the princess!"

Larry-The-White-Horse crawls on all fours as fast as he can and I almost fall over two times.

Finally, we stop at the side of the porch where Princess Connie is twirling a piece of her rope-hair around her fingers and looking bored. She totally forgot to say her lines back to Elizabeth about how she wouldn't marry the old prince even if she had to live forever in the tower.

I climb off of Larry-The-White-Horse and onto the porch.

I kneel on one knee. Looking up at Princess Connie, I say, "Would you be my Juliet?"

Aunt Yola used to say this to me when she'd pretend to be Romeo.

Princess-Stuck-Up Connie doesn't answer.

I clear my throat and adjust my belt and sword which went crooked from jabbing Larry-the-White-Horse in the ribs.

I repeat the question, louder.

"Would you, princess, be my Juliet?"

Princess Connie is shaking and whispers, "Ye . . . yes."

Jesus, Joseph and Mary! She's scared!

I whisper, "Louder, Connie."

Connie, her lip quivering says, "No!"

The audience laughs.

I absolutely feel like killing Connie, but it's a mortal sin, so I'll try to get rid of the feeling.

"You are such a card, princess! I'm Prince Charming Phillip and I've come to get you out of this tower.

"Oh," says Connie.

I whisper, "Give it all you got, Connie!"

Connie looks like she could punch me one.

"Yeah, well how are ya goin' ta climb up here, prince?" Connie says with a smart-mouth attitude.

The audience laughs.

I have to save this play. If I don't I won't be able to show my face outside again. All of my friends will laugh at me.

I take another step towards Connie and I can see the sweat dripping from her nose. The mop must be making her hot.

I have to think of something and think of it fast!

It takes all of my courage. I don't know where the words come from. I hear myself say them and I can't believe what's coming out of my mouth.

"I must find a way, Princess, to get you out of this tower. You are so beautiful. Your eyes are like pools . . . cesspools."

I can tell by the look on Connie's face, a puzzled look, that she doesn't know a cesspool is a big hole under the ground that holds wee-wee and poop.

Aunt Yola used to say funny things like this to me but I never thought I would say it to anybody, especially in front of so many people.

Everybody is laughing and laughing.

I grab a handful of Princess Connie's mop-hair and pretend to start climbing up her hair.

I don't know what comes over Princess Connie, but it looks like a light bulb comes on in her head.

"Cesspool, my Prince?" she says.

"Yes, deep and mysterious, like your beauty," I say making it up on the spot. I continue. "Yes, Princess Connie, even if you were old and ugly, I would save you. Even if you had only one eye, like a Cyclops, I'd save you. It is my job as a Prince to save Princesses."

Connie does a good thing. She stretches out her arms to me like she wants to hug me.

I'm surprised.

Well, I don't know what comes over me except I know I just have to make up stuff. Where this next part comes from, I can blame on Aunt Yola because we used to sing this to each other. I need to get the title of the song I'm about to sing into this conversation.

I stretch my arms out to Princess Connie and say, "Even if I have leprosy, I would come and save you because you are so beautiful."

The audience gasps.

I start singing something that would go with tango music.

> *Leprosy*
> *It's crawling all over me*
> *There goes my eyeball*
> *Right into your highball*
> *Kiss me quick*
> *There goes my upper lip*

I grab Connie and make a big kissing sound in the air.

She throws her arms around me and yells, "My hero!"

I help her get off the ladder so she doesn't trip on her mop-hair.

Everybody is laughing so hard tears are streaming down their cheeks. The audience is clapping and yelling.

Oh my gosh! This isn't the rehearsal. This is the performance!

I hear whistling. It's my Dad who has come home from work and he's sitting on the blanket with Mom and a bunch of other people I don't even know.

Elizabeth yells, "Dats' it, chile. Yo's gots yo man. Lawsy, lawsy! And yo's got the young 'un wit' teeth."

Larry-The-White-Horse is, once again, rolling around on the ground, holding his belly because he's laughing so hard.

Poopie and Robert, the town people, are laughing and pretending to dance. Robert lets go of Poopie and runs on stage and closes the curtain. The audience continues to clap and yell, "More! More!"

Robert opens the curtain. We're all lined up in a row like we had talked about yesterday, holding hands and bending over to bow. I count to three and we all stand up straight. Over and over again, we bow. I shove Elizabeth out front to take a bow. The audience goes wild jumping up and down.

Elizabeth is crying, she's so happy.

I make sure each person has their own time to bow. Connie takes off her wig and the crowd goes wild.

Poopie and Robert hold hands and bow together. They look very happy together. Larry jumps off the porch and starts turning handsprings in the yard to entertain the little kids.

After what seems like ten minutes, the audience quits clapping and they all walk up to the stage.

People I've never seen before tell us how good we are and how we need to put on plays every month.

Many of the moms tell my Mom that they would like to help with costumes and food. Why, even Poopie's mom is shaking hands with my Mom and telling her she'd like to help Mom sew and iron.

Two of Mom's friends ask if Elizabeth is looking for extra work. Elizabeth is hired on the spot.

Dad walks over to me with a big smile on his face.

"Well, ya a good 'un, Dee. Ya did it. Ya great at tellin' stories, just like ya good ol' Dad. Tell me, what do ya think of ya first effort in front of a real audience?"

"Oh, Dad. It was a lot of work, but it was fun. I think I need to learn how to write, so I can write the stories and everybody can stick to the same story. I got really nervous for a few minutes right before the leprosy part.

"Yah, kid, that brought the house down. Ya know, sometimes, Dee, it's good ta fly by the seat of ya pants and take each moment as it comes. It helps sharpen ya imagination."

Dad continues, "So, what did ya learn from this experience?"

"I learned that if somebody, like Elizabeth is just being herself, just let her do it. If somebody's scared, like Connie, try to make that person laugh. If somebody doesn't feel important, like Robert, give the guy an extra job. If someone's mom has a bad opinion of me, I can't help it. And if everybody is driving you crazy, don't get such a bad temper."

"Ya know, kid, that's pretty good advice. Maybe someday ya ought ta write a book or become a politician."

We both laughed.

I take Dad's hand and we don't talk for a few moments.

Finally, I say, "Dad, there's something I want to tell you."

I throw my arms around him and hug him as tightly as I can. Tears stream down my face.

"I'm really glad you came back from the war safely," I whisper.

He strokes my hair for a long time before he whispers back, "Me too, Dee . . . me too."

Afterword

All of the featured relatives, save my cousin, have passed away, but not their splendid spirits. The humor of Mom, Dad, Grandma and Grandpa Steve and my Aunt Yola I recall with love, and I honor their memories. The advice from Grandma Sidoti Canale and Auntie Olympia Sidoti, I still take to heart.

My cousin Pat is still living in New York and is a wonderful mother of her own two children, Christopher and Valerie. Christopher is a father, business owner and Volunteer Fireman in Long Island; Valerie is an award-winning writer who is planning books of her own. Pat takes care of her many pets and loves to create beautiful crafts, knits, and crochets. Much of Pat's working life has been in the service of the elderly.

What fun it was to recount these experiences and to actually see them in my mind's eye, as if I was observing a play from the front row center and these thespians were my relatives. The joy of remembering my Grandmother Catherine speaking Italian, how her hands always smelled of olive oil and how her cooking filled the kitchen with wonderful aromas of garlic, sauces and pastas, brought me back in time to Corona, New York in the mid 1940's.

The kitchen aromas of my father's German parents were very different, but still delicious. Their kind, sweet natures toward me never wavered, nor did their trust that their son, my father, was a young man with a mission in the military.

As I wrote each chapter, I found myself even more submerged in the stories. Many finite details came back to me: the texture of Grandma's silk dresses, the odor of Mom's Coty face powder and Evening In Paris perfume and Dad's shoe polish as he spit-shined his shoes. I either laughed with tears of joy remembering how I learned to dance or wept with tears of sadness as I recalled driving away from the curb at Grandma's house in New York to move to North Carolina.

I miss them all and thank them for the opportunities they gave me to be a free spirit and learn how to live life to the fullest and question what I didn't understand.

I hope all families will encourage their children to act as free spirits as my parents did. However, there were boundaries; they taught me to respect myself and others; there was encouragement to learn and create; there was humor, music and well . . . there was never a dull moment.

I thought I had an unusual childhood until I decided to write my memories for my Granddaughter, Nicole Angelina. As I wrote, I would get reports on Nicole's first tooth, first words, and first steps—celebrated, but not unusual. At the age of fifteen months, she began playing open strings on her violin with the encouragement of her parents who are both musicians. Now it is they who are never having a dull moment.

Imagine what humanity would be like if everyone guiding children would provide opportunities for artistic and emotional growth, while providing boundaries within which they could be creative, respectful and caring.

May we all create an atmosphere to nurture the splendid spirits in all of us, at any age and for all time.

Spirito Splendido

Want To Order More Copies Of Spirito Splendido?

E-mail the Author At DDeevah9@aol.com

Or E-mail Divine Mercy Press At divinemercy@hypersurf.com

Or Write Us At One Of the Addresses On the Copyright Page

We'd Love To Hear From You!